# THE WHITE WITCHES AND THEIR NINE PRECIOUS JEWELS

# THE WHITE WITCHES AND THEIR NINE PRECIOUS JEWELS

## BOOK 1: THE RED RUBY OF BRAERIACH

S.E.AITKEN

First Published by Author Academy Elite 2019
Cover by Andrea Orlic © 2019 S.E.Aitken
Editing by The Guild

Formatting by Jet Launch

The moral right of the author has been asserted in the
Library of Congress, and a catalogue record of this
book is with the US Library of Congress.

**Library of Congress Control Number: 2019912794**

ISBN Paperback 978-1-64085-868-8
ISBN Hardback 978-1-64085-869-5
ISBN E-Book 978-1-64085-870-1

Printed by IngramSpark and KDP

This book is dedicated to

Talia, Niall, Elvy-Rose, My Muse, Stanley, Jolina,
Mum, Dad, Tina, Gran, Gordon and any babies
who are, or will be, part of our crazy clan!
Forever know that I love you all.
You are my heartbeat x

# 1

## How to Bake Magic

The aroma of baking cakes floated through the tiny gap of the station house window. It was a familiar smell which greeted all passers-by at almost the same time each week—a sweet and comforting scent which seemed to embrace and welcome each visitor as they moved through the station on the way to their busy lives. Although the fragrance was something the station visitors had become accustomed to, the odour was incredibly important to the baker. Her name was Ruby Braystoke, and on this day, Ruby was assisted by her excited granddaughter, Primrose. Ruby had baked cakes since she was able to navigate a spoon in a bowl, rattling the spoon around in a beige pottery vessel which carried the cracks of several minor mishaps.

Ruby would inadvertently launch the crock across the kitchen in an ambitious attempt to mix the ingredients because she lacked enough real strength in her delicate tiny arms to follow it through or even hold onto the container. Her grandmother gave her the usual smile and cuddle replacing it with a second pot—also showing similar signs of strain and cracks. A monster tube of glue was permanently at hand, and with a little patience, the bowls were brought back to life in the blink of an eye. The pots had been part of the Braystoke family for almost a century; they might even be referred to as a family heirloom. It had become custom that the females in the Braystoke family learned how to bake together. However, at the time they learned, none of the children knows the importance of the custom. It was only revealed when the time was right. Primrose sampled at least one of the delicious floaty cakes every time she baked but was reluctant to take too much for herself. She knew her Grandma made the cakes for the people at the station in the winter months.

Ruby now a mature lady of forty-seven knew how hard it must be to get up and travel to work on such cold and bitter winter days. So, she wanted to help make things a little easier for them. Each Friday before the sun rose from its bed of clouds, Ruby would walk to the station. She would take a seat, a tartan blanket, a brown table—all light enough for her to carry—and her parcel of special cakes. She would set up the table under the old railway bridge and wait for the travellers to appear. Newer passengers often seemed to be shocked at the appearance of the tiny black-haired lady with what looked like perfectly positioned strips of scorched white hair around her temples and at the bottom of her hair. It looked almost as if the ends of her hair had been dipped into white paint by mistake.

Ruby crouched alone under the old sandstone bridge. When they first saw Ruby, travellers were perhaps somewhat worried about her welfare. However, that passed when she gave a cheery smile and offered the cakes to them. At first, some parents hustled their children away as they did not know Ruby. However, over time, they learned Ruby was a friendly, kind, and harmless lady who could be trusted. They would say hello and sometimes take a cake from Ruby and offer payment or a gift in return. The custom started to become something both Ruby and the passengers looked forward to each week.

Ruby met many new friends this way, and it helped to pass the time. One of the friends she made was Jack. Jack was a young boy who rode the train to school each morning. He would walk by tucked in amongst the other school children. Jack had fair hair and round blue eyes. He carried a blue satchel with his sandwiches inside it. They were in a white plastic box, carefully prepared by his mother each day for lunch. One day, Jack and his mother walked under the bridge, and Ruby overheard the conversation between them.

Jack's mother looked concerned and was talking in a quiet and calm, but firm tone. 'Jack, promise me you will eat your sandwiches today.'

Jack looked down at his shoes and replied, 'Mum, I eat my sandwiches every day.'

Jack's mother shook her head. 'Well, Jack, if you say you eat your sandwiches, I know you tell the truth, so I will believe you, but your dinner assistants tell me you often sit with an empty box at lunchtimes, so, when do you eat them?'

Jack sighed. 'Mum, I eat them at break time before lunch. There is nothing to worry about, I just get hungry earlier.'

His mum looked at him for a second with the concerned look still lingering on her pale, tired face. She pushed her red curls across her ears so that she could look directly into Jack's eyes.

Placing her hand on both of Jack's shoulders, she said 'Okay, well you seem a little thin is all. I need you to be big and strong, so you can be a firefighter like you would want when you are older.'

Jack smiled. 'Don't worry, Mum. I will eat lunch.'

They arrived at the platform, and the train arrived shortly after. They said their goodbyes as Jack ascended the steps to board. The train started to move sluggishly away from the station. As it did, Ruby glanced into the train window at Jack. She was horrified at what she witnessed.

As Jack settled back into the worn green leather seat, the boys behind him unfastened the clips on his blue satchel, lifted out his sandwich box, and took the sandwich. They then returned the box to Jack's bag. Ruby waved her arms to alert Jack to the fact that his sandwiches had been stolen. Jack glanced at Ruby and pretended not to notice. It seemed that not only had he been aware of what the boys had done, but he had also decided to ignore it.

When the following Friday came around, Ruby took up her usual position next to the railway bridge, ready to share some smiles and treats with all her friends at the station. Soon enough, Jack and his mother Penny passed through. Ruby greeted them warmly.

'Hello, Jack. Hello, Penny. What a lovely day it is!'

Jack raced over to Ruby. 'Hi, Ruby. You must be cold today.'

Ruby smiled at Jack's thoughtfulness. It was hard to believe he was only nine.

'Jack, I bring my blanket to keep the chill at bay, and before I leave for the station, I have warm porridge. It warms me from the inside out Ruby continued. 'I think what might keep you warm today is a yummy cake. I am sure there might be space next to your sandwiches. Perhaps you would like two?'

Jack looked to his mother for approval. Penny nodded and was pleased that Jack might be hungry today.

'Which cakes would you recommend, Ruby?' Penny asked. Ruby lifted two cakes from her rickety but immaculately clean gold tin. The cakes were round sponge cupcakes with a black and white magpie sitting on the top. Penny helped place the cakes into the sandwich box, where they appeared to shrink to size before her and Jack's eyes. Both thought this was an illusion since they both felt a little sleepy.

Penny and Jack said thank you and rushed off so Jack wouldn't miss the train. Then, Jack settled into his seat at the back of the carriage. Ruby watched as the two boys behind him once again went to Jack's lunch box. They were delighted at the appearance of such deliciously smelling cakes, almost intoxicated by them they began quickly cramming the cakes into their mouths. Ruby smiled. She was pleased with herself and her clever plan, *that should do the trick*, she thought. Then packed up and left for home.

Benjamin and Neil started to feel unusually tired on the train that morning. They battled with the tiredness as it was only a short trip to their school, and they knew they mustn't miss their stop. Perhaps it was the cakes they had stolen from the lunch box of the boy in front of them. They were extremely filling. The boys felt as if the cakes were growing larger and larger inside their tiny frames with each passing second. The boys were unaware that they had started to nap. The train continued its rhythmic journey, rocking them slowly but surely into a slumber. The boys dozed off so quickly that they were convinced the train had begun to rise into the air, higher and higher. The sea, which usually stretched along the track for the complete length of the journey, was now thousands of miles beneath them. What on earth was happening?

# 2

# The Land of Lost Lunches

'Is that a snake?' Neil screamed.

Both boys were staring at the track beneath them. The rail track now looked like a colossus slithering snake, hissing and spitting as it rippled across the sandy beach. The boys squinted their eyes to look more closely and were alarmed to find the track had, in fact, become a giant snake. Their hearts began to race, and they started to feel scared and confused.

The snake raised its fat bauble-like head from the ground and writhed through the air to the train window. Everyone else had disappeared from the train except Benjamin and Neil. There was no one close enough to hear them as they began to scream. The snake investigated the train window. Although he was a giant snake, he had a warm and friendly face. He smiled a big toothy smile before swallowing the train and the carriage whole—with them in it.

They found themselves in complete darkness. Travelling at the speed of light, faster and faster through the wet slimy insides of the snakes long sticky body. They were going so fast their cheeks were flapping, and they were unable to speak or form words. Eventually, the feeling of movement stopped. The snake burped loudly and then smiled. It catapulted the train out of its body and onto the ground in front of it. Totally dazed, Benjamin managed to let out a slight squeak. 'You okay, Neil?'

Neil's eyes were still wide with terror. 'Not really. What about you?'

'Where are we? What is all of this? Is it real?'

'Looks real enough to me Ben, but if you are dreaming, we are sharing the same dream. The stillness was unsettling after all the previous traumatic events. They looked around them. They were on a sandy plane and the only thing immediately visible was a long and seemingly never-ending street which extended far beyond in the distance. It was hot and dry, and tiny cacti were crowded around their feet. The silence was eventually broken by a thud from behind. A road sign appeared from nowhere.

'Errr Ben, was that road sign there before?'

Ben swung around to look. 'Nope, don't think so.'

They tried to read the sign, but it was virtually impossible. Every time they positioned themselves to read the letters, the sign would move. It was bending and flexing like an elastic band.

Totally perplexed, Ben spoke first. 'We have to find our way back. I thought the sign might have been put there to help, but it does not stay still long enough for us to read it!'

'Why don'ta you ask?' it said in a very unusual accent.

Ben answered, not realising he was no longer speaking to Neil. 'Very funny Einstein. Who would you like me to ask?'

'Ben…I, I didn't speak,' Neil stammered.

The boys heard it again. 'No, but I spoke!'

Both lads swung around and looked at the post, which now had features resembling eyes, a nose and a mouth pinned to its stick-like white frame.

Ben shook his head vigorously as if to rid from his mind any trace of what he was seeing and hearing. 'I am definitely losing it, now a post is talking to me.'

The post stood upright this time and coughed as if clearing his throat in ready to make an announcement.

'If you needa the dough, to the left you musta go, if you needa to go quick, go right but don't slip. If you needa to meat in the middle, follow dis' riddle.'

● ● ●

Ben rolled his eyes. 'Soooo glad I asked,' he said in a sarcastic way.

'Well, it's all we have,' replied Neil. 'Let us at least try to work it out.'

'Fine, but this is nonsense. It does not help any. We still have no clue as to where we are, no matter which way we go.'

The post bent over as if to bow. 'At your service once again. Dat' is easy. You are in the land of lost lunches.'

Ben screwed up his face in frustration. 'Okay, that is it. I have had enough. I am going to the right. If I am going to get mixed up in this, I will take the route which suggests I might get some money.'

'Money?' Neil inquired.

'Yes money. You know, dough? It said dough, it is slang for money. Don't you know anything?'

Ben headed off down the street. Neil reluctantly followed, too afraid to be left alone. Then, almost as quickly as they had made the decision, there was a loud crack of thunder from above. The street began to shake, and the buildings creaked and swayed under the strain of the noise around them. A blast of dust rose from the path on the street. The threatening noise grew louder and closer. They were shocked at what they saw when they looked back. It was an enormous ball of dough rolling toward them at full speed. The ball was quickly closing in on them now. They knew there was no escape. They began to run as fast as their tiny legs would carry them. They tried to get ahead of the ball, but it was pointless. It caught up with them and flopped onto their tiny, wiry frames. It rolled over the top of them, engulfing them and collecting them up with its mighty force, so they became glued to it limb by limb, like a snowball collecting snow. It was the strangest sight. Only their heads and arms could be seen protruding from the dirty, sticky, gooey mess. They rolled for miles and started to feel a trifle dizzy and sick. Then, almost as quickly as the ball had appeared, it disintegrated, leaving them back at the beginning next to the signpost.

'Oh dear, bada move,' said the signpost.

'You don't say,' Ben spluttered while picking out the dough from his mouth and nose.

'Can you perhaps help us a smidgen more this time?' Neil quickly said, in the hope that a kinder, more respectful approach might mean the post was more inclined to help.

'Of course,' the post said politely. 'There are only two other routes left, so picka one. I am afraid you must travel all routes to help find the lost lunches, as I am sure you must know, if it were not for magpie boys lika you, lunches would not get lost, no?'

Neil started to understand. 'Magpies?'

'Magpies,' said the post. 'Magpies are birds which are known to steal shiny things that they like, even when they do not belong to them. You stole lunches, no?'

The friends bowed their heads in shame. It all made sense to them now. They were stuck in this terrible place because they had stolen lunches from Jack. The cakes must have been laced with magic. They began to recall the magpies on top of the cakes. That had to explain how they arrived in the land of lost lunches.

'Okay, I see.' Ben nodded, now resigned to what they must do. 'Let's get this over with then, I vote we meet in the middle this time.'

'It can't be any worse,' said Neil. Ben agreed. Off they went again, this time, separating down adjacent streets as they had planned. Shortly after, they met in the middle, but before they came toe to toe, two enormous men carrying mammoth sized pieces of bread rushed up behind each boy crushing them into a sand-wich. They literally were the meat in the sandwich as the signposts riddle had suggested! Now the boy's cheeks were flaming crimson with anger. Their legs wobbling beneath them threatening to give way. Still covered in runny dough, they were now being shim-mied along inside a gigantic sandwich at breakneck pace. They were jiggling up and down, racing down one road and then the next, twisting and turning for what seemed like hours, until they were returned safely back to the signpost. The men and the pieces of bread quickly and quietly disappeared.

Ben and Neil sat on the floor next to the signpost, exhausted by the whole experience. 'Okay, one last try,' they said at the same time.

The signpost gave a smile and wink. He was really enjoying the game and the boys' company.

'Good luck!'

The only way remaining was right, and hopefully, as the riddle suggested, it would be quick. Off they walked to the right of the signpost and were quickly met by the sound of what they thought was the sea or a swooshing like sound which they had an idea might be running water. They were right. The water was upon them, seeping underneath their feet and sweeping them along. It was then they noticed that the water was warm, sticky and yellow-coloured. It soon became obvious that this was not water. It was butter, as in the butter from a sandwich; it was all over their feet and legs. They were skidding and sliding on waves of butter rushing along each road. They lost their footing several times. First, they were standing, then slipping along until bump!

'Boys, boys, this is your stop,' the train attendant said in a surly manner. They were back on the school train. 'I am not waiting any longer. I have a schedule to meet.'

Neil and Ben looked at each other. Then at their shoes. Then at their clothes. All were clean with no trace of what had happened to them. They looked sheepishly at each other. Neither wanted to ask the other if all of that had really happened. They were too afraid of looking silly or uncool. They both started to talk about it then changed their minds. They decided it was better to try and forget it altogether. They were so glad to be back in one piece from what felt like their worst nightmare. They then remembered the sandwiches and cakes they took from the boy in front and felt pangs of guilt and remorse. There was only one thing they could do, something to try and put things right.

Rising from their seats, Ben said, 'Hi, my name is Ben, and this is Neil.'

They were talking to a boy with fair hair and round eyes seated in front. It was Jack.

Neil said, 'We wanted to say sorry. We sometimes took sandwiches from your bag, and that was wrong. Will you let us share our lunch with you today at school and we will buy you a cake from Ruby as an apology next week?'

Jack was taken aback, but happy. He could use a few new friends and found it in his heart to forgive their behaviour. 'Okay, thank you for telling me. My name is Jack. I would love to share lunch and a cake with you next week.'

They shook hands almost pulling their arms out of their sockets with enthusiasm. Then stepped off the train together and walked to school.

# 3

# The Red Ruby of Braeriach

**B**y now you may have an inkling there was something rather interesting about the cakes the boys took from Jack's lunch box that day. Maybe it was the smell which lured them into eating them and the strange dream-like experience that followed. The cakes had been dosed with an exceedingly powerful type of magic, magic only a witch from the Nine Precious Jewels family could cook-up. Primrose (who also ate some of the cake) did not suffer the same experiences on tasting them. Primrose was born into the family of the White Witches of the Nine Precious Jewels. Ruby was just one of the White Witches, as was Primrose's mother. Each White Witch was named after nine of the most precious jewels in the world!

First, there was Ruby, who was of Scottish descent and still lived on the border of Scotland in a sizable, old house which was once a train station. The front and side windows of the house overlooked the sea. Ruby loved the station house, especially its proximity to the sea. She would often witness all the breathtaking moods of the sea. It could be angry, wild, passionate, calm, placid, serene or content. It was a temperamental being, but it did not matter what mood the sea was in—all were her favourite. Ruby and her family would sometimes call on the sea to help them in some of their more powerful spell making.

•  •  •

Ruby was named Ruby after the precious red jewel widely known for the extraordinary things it symbolizes, such as love, passion, courage and—most of all—good fortune. The name she had been given was no coincidence. Her family always knew she would eventually find out which gemstone she had been named after—the Red Ruby of Braeriach Mountain—and that when she found out, she would be blessed with the stone's extraordinary special and unique powers.

One summer day, (as had been planned by the mystical family long before she was born), Ruby decided to take a long walk. She had been at a loss, looking for something to do and wanted to make the most of the sun. She liked the way it seemed to caress her face with its warm, familiar touch brushing her cares away and making her smile. She walked for what seemed like miles. The ground became steeper and steeper, and although she started to feel weary, this did not deter her from wanting to explore what was quickly becoming some of the highest parts of the mountain of Braeriach. On the ground was a mix of thick green foliage peppered with purple heather. It was prickly in places, leaving scratches on her bare legs which peeped out from beneath her long, grey sack-like dress. The scratching did not stop Ruby. She still clambered up the mountainside, excited at her adventure and what she might find if she reached the top.

At last, the summit was in sight. Ruby raced to reach it with a final surge of energy. However, she tripped on a large, sharp, grey rock and began to roll down the mountain in a direction different from the one that she had walked. Going faster and collecting dust and leaves on her clothes as she fell, she lost all sense of direction and knowledge of where she was. She began to feel scared. She jolted to a stop. She let out a sigh of relief. She was still face down on the earth with her hands and legs splayed around her. She coughed, then bravely opened one eye. The first thing Ruby saw was the rock she had tripped on—it had followed her all the way down and stopped when she had.

'Crazy!' she said.

'Not really' a voice close by replied in a way which sounded like it had a mouth full of marbles. It seemed to be coming from the rock.

Ruby carefully opened the other eye. 'Even crazier.'

'I'll tell you what crazy, dear Ruby is,' said the same odd accent. 'Waiting for twenty years on a mountain-side for you to become bored enough to seek out the exact thing you were meant to find! I mean, I have jaw ache!'

The rock was talking from a mouth in its wrinkly grey face which Ruby hadn't noticed. To make Ruby smile, the rock was imitating her. First, it opened one eye, then the other. Blink, blink, blink went its eyes.

Ruby rubbed her eyes, not believing what she was seeing. 'I am sorry, I don't understand, perhaps I bumped my head in the fall' she replied, not sure if she was talking to herself or a rock.

'Not so' said the rock, and with a cough and a splutter it spat a large red stone out of its mouth. It was a beautiful gemstone, dark red colour like a fresh red rose. Ruby was soon to learn this was her precious jewel, her namesake jewel, the Red Ruby of Braeriach.

Ruby and the rock quickly became great friends. They talked until it was almost dusk. Ruby learned that she was born into a family of witches—all named after precious jewels—and that each would eventually come across their namesake precious stone and learn all about its magic powers. Even more thrilling than that, the witches could use the special powers from the jewel to create white-good-magic! All the precious gemstones were unique with different gifts. White Witches were chosen carefully as having such a powerful jewel was an enormous responsibility. If a White Witch was careless with their jewel, it might fall into the hands of evil, and terrible things would happen. The rock told Ruby that her ruby had many powers. It held magic which could change people's dreams. It could also make people more adventurous. One of its best powers is that it could make people fall in love or become great friends. The jewel was so special that it would protect all of those in its company, especially children. Ruby's eyes grew wide in anticipation of how she might use the ruby.

She squealed with delight. 'Show me, please, show me, rock. How do I use it?' Ruby could not wait to test the stone for herself. 'Will you be part of my first test? I would like us to be friends forever.'

The rock was bursting with pride. 'I would love to be your friend, Ruby. Perhaps you could take me with you and place me in the garden where you live so we can indeed keep each other close and be friends forever?'

Ruby was pleased the stone wanted to be her friend. She gave it a gentle kiss and pat, then placed the ruby in her coat pocket. She was unsure exactly how the magic of the ruby worked, or if it already had, as the rock and Ruby had already become inseparable. She gathered the rock into her arms and started her journey back down the mountain, then paused for a moment. 'Rock?'

'Yes?'

'Do you have a name?'

The rock looked forlorn. 'No, I do not believe I do, Ruby.'

Ruby smiled. 'Then I will give you a name which I think shows how lovely a creature you are. Your name is "Mo Charaid," which means "my friend" in Scottish Gaelic.'

Rock liked the name enormously and snuggled up close to Ruby's arms, feeling enormously safe, warm and protected for the first time in many years.

# 4

## Sylvia and the Pixie King

Ruby and Mo Charaid seemed to float down the mountain effortlessly. The wind engulfed and cushioned them until they reached the bottom.

They were soon walking the winding path towards Ruby's home that she shared with her mother, Amber. The path was not quite a path in that only half of it was furnished with large shiny cobblestones and the remaining half was a dirt track. Ruby's home was a quaint cottage with painted white walls. It had matching white sash windows with wooden frames. They were the type of window you can lift open and push down to shut. The cottage had seen better days and was tired-looking and crooked. Its roof and walls seemed to have bowed with the weather and looked shabby and worn. Roses grew up the wall along-side the front door and some had been battered by the mountain winds.

• • •

Ruby's mother greeted her at the door. Her beautiful, long, dark, and winding curly hair floating on the cool breeze. Ruby noticed how her mother's blue eyes shone when the sun caught them, making them filled with a single drop of water in the bottom of her eye. Her eyes were large and mesmerizing. Amber placed her hands on either side of Ruby's face and gave her a gentle kiss.

'Come inside. You must be cold. I have made some stew. That should warm you through.' Ruby loved her mother's beef stew. It was a welcome hearty meal after her mountain adventure. She kicked off her mud-covered boots and sat down at the table, dodging the crusty hanging steel pans above her head as best she could. The kettle whistled on the black double farmhouse stove. Amber made herself tea and poured a glass of lemonade for Ruby and sat down.

'So, what adventures did the day bring to my beautiful daughter?'

Ruby did not know where to start and wondered if her mother already knew. 'Mother would you believe me if I said I had learned there was something . . . er . . . different about me?'

Amber smiled. 'Perhaps my darling. We are all different and special in our own way; that is how nature intended things. Why don't you tell me why you think you are different?

Ruby pulled the ruby from her dress pocket. 'I found this. Do you know what this is?'

Amber looked at the ruby on the table. It glowed brightly, reflecting on the pans above it. Amber drew her chair back and walked to the wooden chest on the opposite side of the kitchen. She took something from the drawer and returned to the table. She placed two black velvet pouches on the table, each bearing a gold embroidered letter. One read "R" the other "A." She lifted the ruby from the table, placed it into the velvet pouch labelled "R" and pushed it back into Ruby's pocket.

'You must forever keep the jewel in this pouch and hidden, Ruby. The pouch shields the jewel from bad magic. Keeping it hidden means it should not be immediately visible to those who may want to use it for evil.' Amber picked up the other pouch. She carefully took out a bronze-coloured gemstone. 'This is my namesake gemstone, amber. It is not a precious jewel, like yours, but it can still work powerful magic. I found this on a mountain amongst the Panchchuli Peaks in India whilst visiting as a young woman. I stayed in Chaukori with some family friends and, like you, stumbled on the gem and a secret which would change my life forever.'

She squeezed Ruby's hand as Ruby began to squirm uncomfortably in her seat. 'This is nothing to fear, my girl. It is a family blessing. Yes, it makes us different, but it means we have gifts we can use for good and to help ease some of the suffering in the world. This is a real blessing, Ruby, but only if the stones do not fall into the wrong hands. Just as there is good magic, the opposite exists. Part of being a good witch, or a White Witch, is to ensure the stones do not fall into the hands of our enemies who wish to use it destructively to gain power all over the world. That would bring great suffering for many people and living things. Do you understand what I have said so far?'

Ruby nodded silently and remained quiet as her mother continued. 'I have the gemstone amber. It holds some powers, but it is not as strong as the ruby. The reason I have a stone with lessor powers is because of something that happened to my mother, Sylvia— your grandmother. She allowed her gift to pass into the wrong hands.'

Ruby gasped. 'How?'

Amber looked at her hands. 'She was named Sylvia after the precious metal. Her gift was a locket made from silver. One night the locket fell into the hands of Pixie King Vermon. It reached him through the Pixie triplets: P, PP, PPP.'

Ruby giggled at the strange names. Amber raised her eyebrows, smiled and continued. 'King Vermon was the King of all Pixies, ruler of the land of Pixies. They reached the human world through pictures hanging in their houses. They live all around us. An awfully naughty and mischievous bunch of sprights. They are often responsible for the things that go missing in our homes. That is one of the many games they like to play amongst themselves as we sleep. They played the same game one night as Grandma Sylvia slept. Carelessly, Grandma Sylvia placed her locket on her bedside table. She had only just found the locket and placed it there so that it was the last thing she would see as she closed her eyes at night, but the first thing she would see as she opened them each day. She thought this would mean she would know where it was and that it could not go missing. However, as darkness fell around the cottage, the Pixies began their mischief.'

Ruby sat with her chin in her hands fascinated by the story, Amber continued Sylvia's tale…

# 5

# The Silver Locket

'The sun joined her cloud neighbours in the sky as morning arrived. Sylvia felt something that felt like velvet brush her face. It was her cat Ragdoll cat, Princess. She was mostly white with huge electric blue eyes, a black velvet face and soft, fluffy fur. She woke Sylvia each morning in the same way—by gently touching Sylvia's face to let her know it was time to start the day again.'

Ruby interrupted and in an excited manner and said, 'Mother, you have just described our cat, Jasmine.'

Amber mother smiled wisely. 'You are correct, my girl. She is the same cat. Grandma Sylvia loved the cat so much she decided to cast a spell which means Jasmine (or Princess as she was previously known) lives on through the generations. Only her name changed to avoid suspicion.'

Amber drank some tea, then removed the stew dish from the table and walked it to the sink. She was aware she might be overloading Ruby with information. She glanced at her watch. 'I think it may be time for a rest before bed.'

Ruby shook her head quickly. 'No, Mother! Please go on. I am not tired!'

'Very well,' answered Amber. She remembered being equally keen as a young girl to learn about her family. The two talked until the early hours of the morning.

'Not long after the Pixies returned to Pixie Land, Sylvia heard a fantastically strange noise. Princess began to cough on what seemed like a ball of fur stuck in her throat. Hugggh, hugggh, hugggh was the sound she made. Her marble-like eyes almost doubled in size. Then an exceedingly sticky PP launched from Princess's mouth and catapulted across the wooden bedroom floor. Through the night, Princess had noticed the weird miniature creature lurking around the bed and, like most cats, decided it was a toy and proceeded to swallow it whole!

'After Sylvia regained her composure at the sight of a strange, tiny man with brightly coloured clothes (each Pixie wears the same colour as the flower in the picture from which they fell) and a head that looked far too large for his spindly frame, she began to talk to him. "What on earth...what are you?"

'She picked him up by his round mouse-like ears. He was covered in jelly from Princess' mouth. PP was offended and crossed his arms over his chest. With a sulky pout, he said, "What on earth are you? I am a Pixie and proud of it."

'Sylvia looked puzzled. "How did you get into my bedroom? What do you want?"

'PP scoffed at what he thought was a silly question. "I got here because of your dumb cat. All would have been great if she had not caught me."

'Now Sylvia was offended. "If Princess caught you, then you were no doubt up to no good. Princess likes to look after me. What were you doing?"

'PP was reluctant to say why he was in Sylvia's bedroom but made the mistake of looking over at the bedside cabinet. This prompted Sylvia to look over at the same place. Sylvia's eyes widened with horror when she saw the silver locket was missing. She sat back hard onto the bed in dismay. "You did a terrible thing. That was an incredibly precious locket. You must give it back."

'PP shrugged his shoulders and was just a tad ashamed of what he had done. "I don't have it. My brothers do. They have returned it to the Pixie King."

'Sylvia looked sorrowful, and her eyes filled with tears as she began to cry. "I am in so much trouble. Is there any way I can get it back?"

'PP looked at the floor. He was feeling chastened now and regretted being involved in the whole scheme. He knew that the Pixie King and the other Pixies would not give up the locket now, not without a fight. They knew it could be used to create special magic and the Pixie King intended to use it to turn all living creatures into Pixies. The locket had the power to create eternal life and transform living things into other living things. The Pixie world was especially aware of this.

'PP did not know what he could do to help. "I guess they have something you need, but you really don't have anything to offer them or bargain with," he said quietly. Princess rushed forward picked PP up once again in her mouth but dropped him directly into Sylvia's lap instead of eating him. PP was angry now and purple in the face. "Tell her to stop doing that. I am not a toy."

'Sylvia began to understand what Princess was trying to say. She stroked Princess. "Good girl. You are right. He is not a toy, but he *is* something to bargain with. We will tell the Pixie King to return the locket, or we will not return his pocket-sized helper".'

# 6

# Finding King Vermon

'**P**rincess strutted around the bedroom with her tail in the air, looking proud of how she had helped Sylvia to find a way to recover the silver locket. PP was less impressed because the plan involved him becoming a living bargaining tool. He was not confident that the promise of his safe return would be enough of an incentive to force the King want to give back the locket. He was, however, resigned to the fact that this might be the only way. PP was feeling so enormously guilty about the whole situation, so with a heavy heart, he agreed to cooperate in the plan.

'He told Sylvia how she should contact King Vermon using the flower picture. If she held PP's hand, he could push her through the picture using his special powers while he remained in her bedroom. When she was ready to come back, she should ask the Pixies to take her back in exchange for PP's safe return. He promised to hide somewhere in the house just in case the Pixies attempted to find him without Sylvia's help. This plan was his way of apologizing to Sylvia.

'There was no time to waste. Sylvia and PP faced the painting together. They held hands, only releasing once Sylvia had reached Pixie land. The ground was white with large coloured spots on it. It looked like a game of Twister, except each spot was raised like a slight hill. Everything looked as if it had been painted in bright primary colours—there were bright red, vivid yellow and intense blue spots. It was as though the sun was shining, but it did not exist here. Sylvia realised the plan she and PP had devised was not an awfully good one. She neither knew what King Vermon looked like, not where to find him.

· · ·

'There was a popping sound beneath her feet. She saw that a Pixie had popped out from one of the spots on the ground. It was a red spot, and the Pixie was dressed in matching red—including his moustache. Sylvia thought *the spots must be what we know to be houses.* Sylvia wondered whether, if she knew the colour of the Pixie King's clothes, she could find the home that matched? Finding King Vermon would not be easy. The white landscape extended further than her eye could see, and there were many spots of the same colour.

'The red Pixie had noticed Sylvia. It was about to pop back into its spot when Sylvia grabbed its foot. "I'm really sorry. I need to speak with you, Pixie."

'The Pixie was now writhing in Sylvia's hand. "Put me down. This is so extremely uncivilized. All the blood is rushing to my head."

'Sylvia asked the Pixie, "If I put you down, will you stay and talk?"

'The Pixie nodded and gulped several times. He thought it was wise to agree with such a strong and forceful creature. Once he was back on solid ground, he adjusted his crumpled clothing and cleared his throat. "How, er, how can I help you, giant?"

'Sylvia laughed. "I am not a giant. My name is Sylvia, I am a White Witch. I have come to Pixie Land to find King Vermon. What is your name?"

'The Pixie looked somewhat surprised. "My name is Red 108. We common Pixies are named after the spots in which we live. Only royal Pixies are granted real names. You have a vastly ambitious and challenging journey ahead if you wish to find King Vermon. First, you need his address. It consists of spot colours and numbers. To reach him, you must first visit each Pixie in the address line and obtain a stamp. We all act as gatekeepers to one another's homes. It is a neighbourhood watch team of sorts. We make sure the wrong people do not reach the right addresses. The more important an individual you are, the more difficult it is to pass through each spot. Do you still want the address? Do you feel lucky?"

'Sylvia had no choice. She needed to meet with the King and take back the silver locket. "Yes, please."

'Red 108 sighed. "On your head, be it!" He knelt on the floor, rolled up his sleeves and knocked on the ground, whispering King Vermon's name as he did.

'Brightly coloured lights lit up the sky as if reflecting the spots on the ground which were illuminated. There were six and on each of the spots was a number. The lighted spots formed a zigzag pattern across the white ground. "Here is the address, my dear. Good luck." The Pixie popped back into his red spot as quickly as he had appeared.

'Sylvia glanced around; there were seven spots brightly lit—Red 150, Blue 416, Yellow 612, Blue 713, Blue 1002, Green 1100, Yellow 3015. This was King Vermon's address path! She walked to Red 150 first. The distance seemed to increase with each step. Walking was tiring, and her shoes rubbed her feet. Sylvia was also acutely conscious that she was still wearing her long white nightgown. Several hours passed, and she eventually reached Red 150. Sylvia sat down next to the large red hill, then stretched over and knocked on the centre of the spot.

The now-familiar popping noise occurred, and out came a different red Pixie. It was a girl Pixie this time. "Hi, Red 150. My name is Sylvia. I would like to meet King Vermon."

'The Pixie nodded, smiled sneakily and ushered her into the top of the red spot—the hidden door to her home!

# 7

# Pixie Games

'Once Sylvia was inside the spot, she saw that it was a bare and unusual home. It was large and dome-shaped, filled with very little. She stroked the walls with her hand; they felt bouncy like a rubber balloon. Red 150 walked over to a panel in the wall and pushed one of its buttons. The room filled with loud music and a comical ditty. Sylvia listened for a moment to try to catch the words. She was sure it was saying "This is the funky chicken dance." She listened again. The words were instructing her to perform a dance. It seemed the only way on to the next spot was by doing the funky chicken dance.

'The Pixie waved her arms at the space around them. Sylvia was somewhat slow to respond, so the

Pixie began to demonstrate the dance. She bent her arms to imitate chicken wings at the side of her body, wriggled her tail from side to side and bounced her knees at the same time. Then she pushed her head forward and backwards repeatedly in jerky movements as a chicken might. Sylvia tried to stifle her laughter. She reluctantly joined the Pixie in the dance, hoping it would move her on to the next spot as quickly as possible. Her body ached with the effort she put into their funny routine. Sylvia could not really understand why this was necessary for going to the next spot but was sensible enough not to ask. Soon the music stopped. Red 150 shook Sylvia's hand and stamped it with a tiny black stamp which she wrestled from the tiny pocket in her frilly red and white dress. Then, she quietly ushered Sylvia out of the Red 150 bubble.

'Sylvia was back outside, and each of the spots was still lit. She was somewhat confused about what had just happened, but decided not to question it, as it allowed her to move to the next spot. Blue 416 was quite a distance away from Red 150. Onwards Sylvia trekked, reaching Blue 416 sometime later. She was greeted with a spelling test. Blue 416 was a spelling master and used his visitors to test his own intellect. He allowed only one minute per word, testing each visitor with twenty words in total. He was thrilled when words were spelt correctly, and he often spelt away his day.

'The words Blue 416 asked Sylvia to spell were cat, hot, man, van, soup, hand, world, circle, blue, name, family, apple, water, sea, treasure, love, warm, stone, flower and necessary. Sylvia passed the test with only one mistake necessary. However, the Pixie had grown to like Sylvia and kindly gave her a second chance. Sylvia was relieved when she left Blue 416 with a second stamp.

'When she reached Yellow 612, there was another test waiting. This time Sylvia was asked to form sentences using the letters S, T, W, O and P as many times as she could in the same sentence. She paused for thought, then began to speak her answers aloud.

'Although the sentences seemed like nonsense to Sylvia, they seemed to be acceptable to Yellow 612. "The slithering snake slid into the small snug space. The three triplets tricked too many tangerines into tickling toes. The wicked wristwatch wriggled warmly within the water wing. Occasionally oranges over the orizon often open options. Perfect performances present poor painting partners."

'She found the game fun and momentarily forgot her reason for being in Yellow 612. She thanked Yellow 612 for the game. She was beginning her walk to Blue 713 when Yellow 612 began to jump up and down on the spot in a temper. "No, no, no, no, not fair, you twicked me! Orizon, orizon does not begins with Os!"

'Sylvia had not noticed her mistake. "I am so awfully sorry. It was a genuine mistake. Do let me try again. Occasionally, oranges over original olives are often open to options," she said as quickly as she could think it.

'Sylvia thought adding an extra word might please the Pixie and encourage him to forgive her earlier mistake. Yellow 612 smiled, nodded and bowed. He reached into his trouser pocket to retrieve his stamp and stamped Sylvia's arm before waving goodbye.

'Blue 713 was her next destination. On arriving there, she found a young girl Pixie. The game here was one of clapping and chanting. It seemed Blue 713 liked to perform all the clapping rhyming chants you hear on a school playground. She was ecstatic if someone brought a new sequence of clapping or a new rhyme to her door. Sylvia had not played clapping games since school and struggled to remember any. She decided it would be wise to create one.

'Sylvia chanted and clapped. "Two, four, six. Sylvia is in a fix. Get her to the King of Pixies so she can mend it quick. Please, dear Pixie. Take the stamp from your pocket. Press it on Sylvia's arm so she can get the locket."

'She repeated the rhyme three times, all the time leading the clapping sequence in rhythm with the chant. The rhyme pleased Blue 713, as it was new for her too. She gratefully stamped Sylvia's hand and allowed her to pass on to the next spot.

'Blue 1002 was soon close by, and this time Sylvia was challenged to a tap-dancing test. Blue 1002 was also a young female and had shoes prepared and ready for Sylvia to wear. She had shelves full of different dance shoes—ballet, tap and modern. After Sylvia had placed the shoes on her feet, Blue 1002 demonstrated the steps and asked Sylvia to follow each move separately first, then join the steps together in time with the music. Sylvia was not a natural dancer and did not get the steps at first, but she tried until eventually, she was able to imitate the dance in the way that Blue 1002 had demonstrated.

'Blue 1002 stamped her hand, and Sylvia was on her way. She was starting to feel hungry and exhausted, but her panic over the missing locket gave her the strength to keep going. Then, as if the Pixies had planned it this way, she faced the most difficult test since the start of her journey. Upon reaching Green 1100, she was surrounded by five male Pixies. Each Pixie wore fencing attire and masks. They were dressed in green with black chestplates for protection from any swords which might cause injury. They drew their swords simultaneously and challenged Sylvia to a fencing fight. A sword was waiting in a sleeve in the ground in front of Sylvia. Sylvia had never held a sword and did not want to hurt the Pixies or herself.

'She knew the rules and that she must abide by them if she was to continue. The Pixies launched into attack mode. They were extraordinarily quick on their feet, nimbly spinning and chopping their swords through the air and almost reaching Sylvia. Sylvia's heart was racing, and her hands were sweaty. She gripped the sword with all the strength she had. Fortunately, Sylvia was much taller than the Pixies with a longer reach so she could see them all at once and anticipate which Pixie would move next and how.

'She handled the sword with grace and elegance in an almost choreographed dance. Sweeping it in front, from behind her body on occasion, and up and down. An onlooker would not have guessed she had never held or used a sword before that day. To make her final point, she gently knocked all the Pixies to the floor. She wanted to show them that she could have created more harm if she had not been born with such a gentle and compassionate nature. Each Pixie was grateful for the tough but invaluable lesson. After they brushed the dust off their clothes that had collected while rolling around on the floor, one Pixie stepped forward and spoke.

'It seemed strange to Sylvia, as the other Pixies had rarely spoken, and she was unsure if they could speak her language. "Congratulations, Sylvia. You have passed all our tests. We have pushed you to the point of exhaustion. Then we provided you with a means to hurt us—the sword—which was to test your heart and to see if, when pushed to your limits, you would harm any of our Pixies. As you did not, we are willing to take you to our King and are confident he will be safe in your company." Then the Pixies vanished.

'Sylvia felt the puzzle pieces falling into place. Everything made sense. The games, the dances—they were all a way to make Sylvia tired enough so that when she reached the sword fight, she might be especially angry and misbehave.

'Sylvia shouted, "No, wait! How do I get there!?' Her shout was met by silence. Sylvia looked around and saw the final yellow spot still illuminated. She knew no other way to find the King, so she continued with the original instruction—follow the spots.

'She ran with her last bit of strength to reach Yellow 3015. Gasping for breath, she came to her destination. She rapped on the door. However, this time the spot started to grow, swelling and stretching high into the sky, effortlessly pushing anything in its path to one side. The spot began to change shape. Sylvia rubbed her eyes and realised she was looking at a beautiful golden yellow palace.

# 8

# King Vermon's Palace

'**S**ylvia was astonished at the sight of the majestic golden palace. She was nervous and intimidated, feeling insignificant next to its glory. She walked closer to the enormous door, which was made of solid gold. Before she reached the door, it began to drop slowly to the ground. It was suspended on a set of strong golden ropes. At least a hundred Pixie guards appeared in the courtyard, all dressed in their usual bright colours with matching tunics, boots and tall golden military-like helmets.

'The guards appeared calm and were motionless as Sylvia walked past them. She entered a doorway to a large hallway with shiny gold marble floors. There was a staircase on the other side. She glanced to the top of the stairs to see a Pixie dressed in fur robes and wearing a crown that almost touched the ceiling. The Pixie's neck was heavy with jewels and necklaces; even his boots were encrusted with shiny gems. She looked closer and saw that one of the necklaces seemed extremely familiar. It was her silver locket!

'Sylvia performed a curtsey as she knew she must now be facing King Vermon. The Pixie King spoke first. "Welcome, Sylvia. I have been watching your journey and trials with great interest. You performed the tests exceptionally well. However, I think your efforts are in vain. I know why you are here, but I do not have any intention of returning the silver locket to you. Why would I?"

'Sylvia had not expected the King would immediately return the locket as he knew of its powers. "King Vermon, why is the locket so important to you? It is not rightfully yours. It belongs to me and is a family treasure, greatly loved and cherished. You should return it."

'The King laughed loudly, his deep voice echoing around the walls of the great hallway. This was unsettling for Sylvia. "If it is so loved by you, Sylvia, why were you so careless with it?" The King looked smugly at his nails as if to appear disinterested in the conversation. "The locket will stay with me. I will use it to strengthen and increase my powers by making more Pixies who will serve me. We will eventually take over the world." He sneered at the last few words and a look of power and greed crossed his face.

'The King was dreadfully intimidating; however, she was determined not to leave without the locket. She had come too far. She cleared her throat. "King

Vermon, you are a bad man. The locket does not belong in hands that will use it for evil. Return the locket or I will not return your beloved PP."

'*There*, she thought. *I said it*. It was not in her nature to threaten the safety of such a tiny creature; however, PP had helped her come up with the plan and was willing to follow through with the plan as an apology to Sylvia.

'King Vermon regained interest in the conversation. He walked quickly down the stairs towards her. He was so close she could feel his breath on her face. "If you have my PP, you had better return him, or I will cause chaos in your home." This time he was snarling.

'Sylvia took a few steps back to regain her composure and confidence. "King Vermon, I will not return PP until you return the locket. Whatever you decide to take from my home will not be of the same value as the locket and will only bring attention to your existence, which I feel sure is something you do not want to do. Humans will capture you and conduct experiments on you to try to understand what you are and how you are made. Horrible experiments on your kinfolk in laboratories."

'The King's face grew exploded with anger. He realised he might not hold as much power as he thought. "Very well, you can have the locket this time, but I will return and take it from you. You will never rest or sleep from this day forward." Then he smiled "You should also know that I began my work already. The guards you saw at the gate. They used to be wood-louse. I created more of my people using the locket. My empire is becoming larger and stronger. Look and learn" He waved the locket once more and a tribe of miniature woodlouse appeared before their very eyes. Then, like a spoiled teenager, he took the locket off and threw it over his shoulder in Sylvia's direction as he walked back up the staircase. Sylvia scrambled for it and placed it around her neck. She turned on her heel and ran like the wind all the way back to the dot from which she came.

It seemed to take days to reach the original dot. Her clothes now crumpled and clad with dust. Sylvia fought to find a last ounce of strength before reaching her original starting point. Fueled by the desire to return to her home and family she loved, as well as her need to follow through on her original bargain with the King. She must return PP—this kept her going. She found the dot where she entered Pixie Land and pushed her hand into the flower head, hoping PP could see it on the other side. After around a minute, she felt a tug from the other side and was pulled safely back into her bedroom.

'PP smiled. He could see their plan had worked. He was ecstatic that he could return home. "I hope King Vermon is not too mad with me," he said.

'Sylvia smiled. "He is your family. Family always forgives family; that's how it is. You should go now. Hurry back. Thank you for helping me, PP. I will never forget your kindness." They wrapped their arms tightly around each other like old friends that may never meet again. Sylvia would really miss this little puck. She hoped one day their paths might cross under better circumstances. PP pressed his hand against his lips and blew a kiss her way. Then disappeared back into the flower in the picture frame.

# 9

# Queen Diamond's Punishment

The candles had almost burnt out in the kitchen. Ruby was captivated by her mother's story. Amber knew she should probably stop now and allow Ruby some sleep, but she remembered all too well how at the same age was compelled by the same story and its importance in making sense of her own life.

'Phew, so the locket was returned safely, and everything was as it should be?'

Amber shook her head in response. 'Not quite, Sylvia had made a terrible mistake in leaving the locket visible. Worse, the locket had been used for evil. In the world of White Witches, this did not go without a consequence.'

Amber recounted the tale of woe.

'The Queen of the White Witches in those days learned of the night's events. Her name was Queen Diamond, and she was a strong, striking woman with beautiful fair hair. She was tall with long slender legs and wore a white chiffon dress with sequins littered all over it. The sequins stopped at her neckline and made it appear as though she wore a diamond necklace around her throat. She appeared at Sylvia's bedside soon after she heard the news. Sadly, she had no choice but to reduce Sylvia's powers so they could never fall into the wrong hands again. She allowed Sylvia to keep the locket but told her it could no longer be used for magic. Queen Diamond was sorry to do this but told Sylvia it was the safest thing for both the human world and Validor. She did, however, allow Sylvia one last use of the locket.

'Queen Diamond asked Sylvia, "If you could change the path of one last living thing, who or what would it be?" Sylvia knew instantly that she wanted to make sure that Princess was immortalized and lived forever so that all witches could have a clever and beautiful cat in their company the way she had. Queen Diamond granted Sylvia's wish. Queen Diamond had one more thing to do; she had to make sure that any children Sylvia might have would not have too much magic at their disposal. The White Witches believed if a Witch had been clumsy with their gifts it was unlikely, they would be able to parent a child with the same gifts in a way which would ensure the world was safe from harm.

'Queen Diamond told Sylvia that although she would have a child, the child could not have a precious jewel. Instead, she could have a gemstone which had some powers, but none as strong as those of a precious jewel.

"Sylvia, your child will have an amber stone. The stone will mean your child can heal people, calm people and increase their intellect and wisdom temporarily. It will be a pretty honey-coloured stone."

'Before she left Sylvia, Queen Diamond reminded her about the importance of protecting the locket and stone. She told her to find a better way to keep it out of the wrong hands. One-week later Sylvia had lovingly stitched together two black velvet pouches, one for her locket and the other in ready for the amber gem. When I grew old enough to understand, I learned from my mother's failing and made an identical pouch to hold your stone when it came time.'

• • •

Ruby was now of White Witch age, which was exactly thirteen years, thirteen months, thirteen minutes and thirteen seconds. In human years she would be fourteen years and one month old. When a new White Witch becomes aware of who she was and that there was a wider white family, other White Witches were keen to make themselves known and welcome the new White Witch into the family.

The Witches called a White Witch Sept meeting. It was a meeting which had many purposes—celebrations, decision making, spell casting and on rare occasions barring a White Witch from the White Witch community (which only happened when a White Witch used her powers for dark deeds).

Amber asked Ruby if she felt ready to attend the White Witches Sept.

'Yes, I am, but could Mo Charaid join us too?' Ruby remembered her new friend Mo Charaid, who had been quietly listening to the story from inside her pocket. She took him out and placed him on the table. 'He is my new friend and protector!'

Amber was not quite sure what the rock was, or from where he came, but any protector of her daughter was welcome in her home.

'Absolutely! Now, we must sleep and prepare the house and ourselves for the meeting of the Sept tomorrow.'

They rose from the table and headed up the stone stairway to their bedrooms. Jasmine was waiting on Ruby's bed for her and looked pleased. Ruby was both nervous and excited and started to feel part of something fantastically special and powerful. She felt incredibly lucky to be part of such an important family and vowed to learn from Grandma Sylvia's mistake and keep her ruby safe and close to her. Although she had learned so much about her family, she felt there was still so much to learn. She hoped meeting the other witches would help her answer some questions she had.

She began to consider what she might wear. *What do White Witches wear?* 'What should I wear?' Ruby shouted across the corridor between her own and her mother's bedroom.

Amber laughed. 'Time to sleep, my angel. You must be fresh for tomorrow's festivities. I will help you with a dress and all that you need tomorrow. Do not worry!'

Ruby gave Jasmine a gentle stroke and placed Mo Charaid on the floor next to the foot of her bed. None of them really understood what was happening, but the feeling in the room was that it was something truly magical. Jasmine rubbed herself against Ruby's leg. Ruby gazed at Mo Charaid. He looked strong and rugged like a little warrior stone and although her hands had begun to shake a little in anticipation of what might happen. She felt safe.

# 10

# A Message in the Stars

R uby pulled back the curtains, and the sun streamed into her bedroom, lighting up the room and her soul. She was looking forward to the Witches Sept later this evening and was ready to help her mother prepare the house. She hurried downstairs. Amber was already up and busy in the kitchen. There were pots and plates scattered everywhere with different food in them.

'How can I help?' Ruby asked.

Amber asked Ruby to begin cleaning around the house and open the windows for the fresh air to pass through. It had been quite some time since the house had any visitors and although witches are not known to be clean and fussy creatures, White Witches were the opposite. They liked things clean, precise and perfect. The house must be spotless. Ruby and Amber worked together, scrubbing, polishing, sweeping and mopping. Even Jasmine helped by chasing cobwebs out of the corners of each room. Meanwhile, in the kitchen, Amber had prepared many delights. Not the frogs' legs and bat wings you might expect for a witches meeting; instead, it was a banquet for a king—or for White Witches!

There was roast beef, tender chicken, pork with crackling and succulent vegetables all colours of the rainbow whose scent floated through the air creating a delicious aroma. There was fresh seeded bread, fruit and cakes (the family speciality). The cakes were spectacular—all shapes, colours and sizes, none of which could be designed and created by the human hand. In the garden, large cauldron-like barrels were filled with juice which was a special punch with floating fruit dancing around the surface. Amber referred to this as White Witches brew. Gripping onto the side of the cauldron were tiny silver goblets. As if by magic, the goblets literally clasped onto the side of the cauldron in a most bizarre manner. Ruby tried to prize one away but could not. She decided to leave it to the experts when they arrived.

Ruby felt sure they must be close to being ready to receive their guests when she remembered she had not washed or changed. She walked to the bathroom and began to draw a bath. They had a large white freestanding bathtub with copper taps. The water slowly trickled in until the tub was full.

Amber passed through the hallway and caught a glimpse of the bath. She joined Ruby in the bathroom and took a glass bottle from the only shelf in the bathroom, it was full of bath crystals. Amber opened the bottle and tipped its contents into the bath. The bath hissed at first, then started to sparkle and shimmer like a thousand diamonds. Ruby was stunned but quickly slipped off her nightdress. She dipped one foot and ankle into the bath. It was a little hot, so she took it back out. As she did, she noticed that her foot and ankle were now shining as though made of glass.

'Don't panic,' Amber said. 'This is all part of the ceremony. You should be the brightest belle of the ball.' Ruby nodded and concentrated on getting into the bath. After she had washed, she stepped back out. Her body was now glass-like and translucent. She shone like she imagined an angel would.

Amber returned to the bathroom with Ruby's dress. All White Witches wore white robes, but each had a subtle difference. Whichever stone the Witch owned would be visible on certain parts of their attire. In Ruby's case, she had red heart-shaped stones running up each sleeve and through the centre of the corset-like bodice. She had light chiffon sleeves that were designed to stay on or off the shoulder. They had frills around the top and bottom. Amber passed Ruby a shoebox. Inside the box was a high-heeled ankle boot with many straps running across the foot and ankle to reveal sparkly and pretty peep-toes. She began to dress Ruby's hair, which was long and dark, with the signature white streaks running from her temples past her ears. The white streaks had been there since Ruby was a baby. Amber created a low ponytail with twists at either side, and each twist was pinned with tiny red flowers. Amber's outfit was similar in that it was white, but she had yellow stones trailed around the hem of her dress and sleeves. Her dress was simpler than Ruby's. Finally, as a finishing touch, Amber tucked a delicate crown into the folds of Ruby's hair.

Mother and daughter walked to the long mirror together and admired their work. They gave each other a loving embrace. They were ready.

Ruby asked, 'How will the other White Witches know where to come and what time should we expect them?'

Amber replied, 'They have received invitations already. If a White Witch points her stone at the correct stars in the sky, she can message the witches. Each star represents a letter. Only White Witches can use this form of communication. The other White Witches can read the message in the stars.'

Ruby was amazed. 'Like text messaging, you mean. But what if they are not looking at the sky?' Ruby asked.

'The message will stay in the sky until the witch that created it deletes it. She deletes it in the same way she created it—by revisiting each letter and if she so wishes she can start a new message.' Amber took Ruby outside to show her the message which was still showing in the sky. 'They will be on their way but will only arrive in the thirteenth hour, thirteenth minute and thirteenth second. That's thirteen minutes past one am to humans.' Together they watched the stars in the sky. Their arms tightly around each other's slender frames until the thirteenth hour was upon them.

# 11

# The White Witches Sept

The roar of car engines filled the air as each witch arrived. Ruby was astonished as she looked around the garden at the cars parked in a semi-circle around the house. It was as if they were providing a protective barrier between the real world and theirs. There was a white Lamborghini Huracan which belonged to Pearl, a green McLaren 650s which belonged to Emerald, a blue Porsche 918 Spyder for Sapphire, a black Ferrari LaFerrari for Opal, a grey Lamborghini Venono for Alexandrite, an orange and black Bugatti Veyron Super Sport for Moonstone and finally, for Morganite a pink Zenvo STI. Ruby thought *They must be some of the fastest cars in the world.*

The White Witches had extravagant taste. The secret is that they never needed to spend any money. Among them, they could use magic to create almost any lifestyle or home they wanted. Even the cars (although they looked and sounded like traditional cars) were powered by magic. Amber's tastes were a little simpler. She did not use a car and lived amongst the mountains in Scotland. She wanted to be far away from a society she felt she did not fit. The life she had was enough for her. Strangely, when the time came for Ruby to find her own place in the world, she also chose a humbler life in Cumbria in a station house next to the sea.

The noise of all the cars together was deafening. Amber and Ruby placed their hands over their ears. Amber turned around and walked back into the house, muttering, 'Showoffs.'

Ruby stayed to greet the witches. They looked magnificent. Morganite was first up the path. He wore a white trouser suit with a long flowing jacket, little pointed boots and a trilby hat with a pink diamond-encrusted sash and bow. He had short hair, shaved close to his head, and his make-up was glamorous, almost a work of art.

'Hello, I am Ruby.'

Morganite smiled. 'Hello, Ruby, darling. I am White Witch Morganite from Brazil. Nice outfit. Careful with too many frills, though. Always unflattering to the arms, I find.' He straightened his hat, replaced his lipstick, held his head high so he could see out from beneath the brim of his hat and walked gracefully into the house.

The next in line was Moonstone, who was dressed in a fitted, short, white lace dress with a white lace cape lined in orange silk. She wore white stilettoes and had shoulder length, fiery red hair that nearly matched the orange in her cape.

'A pleasure,' she said, holding out her hand for Ruby to shake. 'I am White Witch Moonstone.' Ruby shook her hand and Moonstone continued down the path.

Alexandrite followed, dressed in a white linen trouser suit and a grey tee-shirt tucked loosely into his pants.

'Hi, Ruby. Thank you for the invite. Great night for it,' he said as he walked by.

Pearl walked up wearing a tight white polo style jumper, white leggings and white over-the-knee boots. She had a large Pearl cameo on the neck of her jumper and a large silver Pearl bracelet. Her hair was as black as night, and her skin was pale. She bowed her head as she reached Ruby.

'Hello. I am White Witch Pearl from China.' Following her introduction with a strained smile.

Next was White Witch Sapphire, who wore a white short-sleeved dress with a wide blue silk ribbon threaded through it. She wore a round hat. Sapphire was larger in size than Pearl and had beautiful dark skin.

'Hi there, Ruby. I am White Witch Sapphire from Africa. Welcome to the family. Now give me a hug.' She folded Ruby into a warm embrace, almost crushing her in the process. Ruby was pleased Sapphire had felt free to hug her. She had a big booming voice and personality to match. Ruby thought she looked like fun.

Opal was next in the procession. Opal was in white shorts, white fluffy ankle boots and a white slashed tee-shirt. She had on a white denim jacket with black stones stitched into it. The same stones were on her tiny white cowboy hat which was pinned to her hair on one side. Her hair was blond with flashes of black stripes across it. It was long on one side and shaved on the other. She looked like a rather eccentric character. She slapped Ruby on the back.

'Just checkin' in. White Witch Opal from Australia.' She smiled a sticky smile, showing the chewing gum in her mouth. Ruby returned the hello and awaited her last guest, White Witch Emerald. Emerald had on a white toga-like dress with a heavy gold necklace collar. The necklace had green emeralds intermittently situated between each chunky gold link. She had shoulder-length straight dark hair with short fringe. She had cat-like eyes, and dark exotic skin. She walked quickly towards Ruby.

'Ruby, I presume. I am White Witch Emerald from Egypt. Let's get this over with,' she said in a no-nonsense sort of way.

Ruby followed the witches through the house and into the back garden. Some of them were in conversation with each other. Others were sampling the punch drink from the large gold ornate cauldrons. Morganite was cleaning the garden furniture with a tissue before sitting on it. Sapphire was studying him--not quite believing what she saw. She shook her head in despair and laughed a deep belly laugh.

'Sit yourself down,' she told Morganite. Morganite disregarded the comment and kept cleaning the chair until he felt he could sit on it. Opal and Moonstone were clinking punch glasses and dancing to music which had started to play seemingly from nowhere. Ruby felt sure the witches had something to do with its origin.

Amber appeared from the house then whispered into Emerald's ear. 'Shall we make a start?'

'Indeed,' replied Emerald as she stood in the centre of the White Witch seating circle which had started to form in the garden. 'Let's do this,' she said enthusiastically.

# 12

## The White Witch Sept Ceremony

Ruby was overwhelmed by the whole event but pleased that all appeared to have literally moved heaven and earth to be there. They looked an incredible and formidable bunch. Their clothes were all the colours of the rainbow that matched their unusual and colourful personalities. Ruby knew that this unusual mix of people would make for an exciting and spectacular night. She did not know what to expect but knew that whatever was to come, it would be extraordinarily special. Her mother had explained that each witch had unique and special gifts. The gifts they had been blessed with were determined by the power within their namesake stones. During the ceremony, each witch would demonstrate one of their gifts, which would be their way of introducing themselves and provide the opportunity for the new White Witch to memorise the other witches' powers. They knew the knowledge of this might be useful to the new White Witch in the future.

Amber did not take part, as she was the host, so no introduction was required. Another reason for this is that Amber was the only White Witch who did not carry the name of a precious jewel. Amber was a gemstone. Amber's mother, Sylvia, had sacrificed some of her daughter's powers when she temporarily lost her stone to the Pixies. Sylvia had accepted the reduced powers as she felt she had let the coven down in a moment of stupidity and did not want the additional responsibility. She was worried that she might make the same mistake again. Amber was content to admire the gifts of her White Witch family and now those of her daughter.

The party had really started to rock. There was music, laughter, eating and drinking. The White Witches knew how to welcome a new White Witch to the Sept. Any new member provided a renewed energy and a sense of purpose amongst them. It strengthened their magic as a collective and meant they could provide more help to those in need. Most importantly, it increased their power against the darker forces.

Ruby danced and was passed around the Witches. Manicured hand to manicured hand. Blue nails, green nails and white nails. It made Ruby quite dizzy. She grinned from ear to ear, and her cheeks hurt. She was on cloud nine, and totally uplifted. She wished the night would never end. It was a warm night with no wind, perfect for such a joyous occasion. They were surrounded by floating fires and candles that moved in time with the music. At first, it seemed a little strange, but Ruby soon became accustomed to it, as well as other peculiarities.

Even Jasmine made a guest appearance. She was fascinated with the flying candles and attempted unsuccessfully to bring them to the ground several times. After many failed attempts, some singed whiskers and an injured bird (who was inadvertently caught in the failed candle massacre), the cat gave up the fight. Eventually, the candle disappeared almost as quickly as it had appeared, giving Jasmine a sense of accomplishment. She did not notice that all the fires and candles had disappeared.

The air filled with the sound of slow rhythmic drums echoing through the night sky. That was the signal for each witch to step forward to perform their introductory ritual.

Alexandrite was first into the centre of the circle of chairs. Although they had performed such shows in the past, the order of the introductions was traditionally in alphabetical order. Alex began to dance slowly and sensually to the drumbeat. He stretched up, then dropped down, up and down, up and down, then stretched up high again with his hands outstretched towards the moon and stars. He stroked and caressed the air using weird but fascinating hand movements. Ruby was mesmerised by the movements. Alex

59

stretched out his arms one final time, then opened his mouth wide and fell to his knees.

Ruby saw a star flash across the sky, growing closer and closer as it did. In a flash, the star had moved into Alex's mouth and was still visible as it travelled down his torso and rested at waist height. Alex's eyes remained closed until the star came to a halt. He had swallowed the star! His eyes sprung open and shone bright grey like a mirror. Ruby was astounded. Precious jewels all have specific properties or special powers. Alexandrite carries the power of empowerment. It can provide a thing (or person) with the ability to do things they might not ordinarily be able to do. Alex walked over to the bird Jasmine had so carelessly knocked to the floor earlier. It was still visibly disorientated, staggering around the floor as if it didn't know where it was. Its wings were limp.

Alex quietly knelt next to the bird so not as to startle it. He lifted it from the floor, carefully cradling it in both hands. He leant forward and let out a breath of air, covering the bird's entire frame with warm breath. He closed his mouth. The bird remained still for a few moments, then began to push itself to stand. It was no longer rocking. It turned to look at Alex as if to thank him. Then it departed by lifting its repaired wings and flying into the night sky. The wings were surrounded by tiny sparkling lights, shimmering as they flapped.

The Witches shrieked with excitement. They never grew tired of witnessing Alex's gift. Ruby gasped in disbelief. She was honoured to have witnessed such a magnificent occurrence and proud to be a member of this world of magic. She could not wait to see the other blessings the other witches carried.

# 13

# White Witch Blessings

Alex stepped to one side and in a gentlemanly way, offered his hand to the mysterious Emerald. He led her to the space he had previously occupied to allow her to begin her own introduction. Emerald's eyes were as green as the emeralds that adorned her outfit. They glinted, reflecting the floating baubles which had circled around the party since it had commenced. She was a quieter member of the family, although her quietness should not be interpreted as weakness.

Emerald was a White Witch with a strong sense of right and wrong. She was known for her firm but fair nature. Her straight but angularly cut hair gave her a mysterious and intriguing look. She was never surrounded by friends because she found it difficult to trust anyone; this was one of the downsides of her special gifts.

Alex began to step away from Emerald. Before he was able to let go entirely, Emerald gripped his hand more tightly. Alex pulled hard, trying to escape her vice-like grip. Emerald spun around and looked him directly in the eye. Alex was starting to feel somewhat uncomfortable, and a trifle scared. The drums stopped, and Emerald spoke.

'Why?' She cupped Alex's face in her hands. 'Why did you do it?'

Alex was now totally confused. 'Excuse me?'

Emerald leaned closer to his face. 'You were not true to Pearl. You kissed another girl.' Pearl blushed, which instantly showed in her pale cheeks.

Alex said. 'In my own defense, we were only seven years old!' He was a little perplexed that such a seemingly insignificant thing had even been mentioned.

Emerald shook her head in disappointment. 'Pearl's heart was broken at such a young age.'

Alex was dumbfounded. How could Emerald have known such a thing? 'How could you possibly know that? We never told anyone or discussed it again.'

Emerald smiled. 'I see into the hearts of men and women. I see good and bad. I see secrets long buried or as fresh as the day they came into being. There is little that can be hidden from me.'

Ruby noticed Emerald's eyes had changed colour throughout her display. Her eyes had become murky grey as if they had become somehow tainted by what they had seen. Emerald let go of Alex's face and shuffled back to her seat. She sat down, ready for the next introduction.

Moonstone rose from her seat, rhythmically swinging her hips confidently from side to side. She walked past the other witches in her figure-hugging white dress, her red hair slightly lifting in the breeze. She walked directly over to a large plant pot full of soil. On the surface of the soil, a flower peeped through. The flower looked to have been battered by wind and sea air. Moonstone lifted the plant pot a little awkwardly as she was slight and weak. She carried it cautiously to the middle of the circle and placed it on the ground with a thud. She positioned her hands over the top of the pot, and the sound of a harpsichord began to chime through the air. After a few moments, the flower began to grow. It was pushing its way through the gaps in her fingers. Then more flowers followed in quick succession. The plant pot soon began to overflow with perfectly beautiful white flower heads stretching their tender stalks to face the sun.

Ruby was astounded. Moonstone had the power to heal, perhaps even to create a new life. The other witches clapped and shrieked in joy. Moonstone took one of the white flowers from the pot and broke the stem. She placed the flower into Ruby's hand and closed her fingers around it, then clenched Ruby's hand within her own. After a moment, flowers could be seen emerging through the cracks in her finger's. They forced their way through without any real effort. The witches responded with even louder clapping. Moonstone removed her hands and performed a humble curtsy. She started the walk back to her seat, but before reaching it, she tripped and landed face down on the stone floor.

Alex lifted her properly to her feet. 'Moonstone, you really do know how to make an entrance.'

Moonstone tried to cover her clumsiness with an equally clumsy lie. 'Yes, it's part of the show. It adds drama, you know, makes it more interesting' She was trying to dress the fall as intentional, intimating it was designed to make the show more enjoyable. They all knew this was not the case but allowed her to continue with the story to keep her dignity. They were used to her clumsy nature but loved her more for it. She straightened her dress and hair and sat down on the floor close to where she landed.

Morganite was next. He was ostentatious, flamboyant and loud, and a little theatrical in personality. He waved his hands in the air, and the harps stopped. He then produced two wands and began to wave them in the air as if conducting an orchestra. Band music began to play. It sounded like a mix of jazz and blues, and a splash of saxophones and bass working in harmony, creating a lovely melody. He turned to face the mountains to the rear of Amber's house. They were stunning, majestic and proud as they rose from the landscape. Sharp jagged ridges huddled together as though shielding one another from the worst weather. They were smothered with wildflowers in blues, yellows and purples.

Morganite pointed at his eyes, then to everyone else's eyes, signalling to them that they must watch. They all turned to face the mountains and saw two people. They looked tiny due to their distance from

the group and were on opposite sides of the mountain. It appeared one was male the other female. Both
appeared to be unaware of the other's existence. It was
not clear how or why they were there. However, what
happened next meant their lives would change forever.

Morganite produced a clear ball from his pocket.
He let out a breath of air which, upon leaving his
mouth, took the form of a snake. The mist snake circled the crystal ball, twisting and turning around it.
Soon the mist began to dissipate into tiny dust-like
particles dispersing into the air. Then the crystal
ball began to grow until it reached almost six feet in
height, almost the same height as Morganite himself.
Morganite passed the wands across the ball, crossing
and uncrossing. The couple could now be seen through
the glass walls of the ball. It was like watching through
a television screen. They were still on opposite sides of
the mountain. The girl looked to be around twenty and
was wearing a green wax coat, blue jeans and brown
walking boots. The boy looked similar in age but wore
sports shorts and a matching shirt with spiked trainers.
Morganite pressed the wands to his lips to signal that
they should remain silent.

He spoke out loud. 'West.' The couple responded
by pausing for a moment. It was as though Morganite's
instruction had become a thought in each of their
minds. Each changed direction and turned to the west.
It was not too long before they were only steps away
from each other.

Morganite spoke again. 'Love.' He blew on the
crystal ball. All the Witches wore confused but inquis-
itive expressions at this point. Curious about what

Morganite was trying to achieve until they say the two individuals began talking as if they had known each other all their lives. They laughed and walked together, touching and holding hands.

Morganite understood that in order to demonstrate his gift, he would need to move forward in time, so he crossed his hands and said, 'Two years, five years, ten years.' The crystal began to spin, and the images in it appeared to move rapidly, as if on fast forward. Scene after scene passed, snapshots of the couple's life that would be. Romantic meals, more walks, a wedding proposal, holidays, their wedding and children. It was an inspirational display of the power of love—or rather, the power of Morganite!

Morganite was pleased with his achievement and felt that was enough of a demonstration of how he could make the world a better place through his gifts. The witches oohed and aahed, clapping at the lovely display of Morganite's gifts. Some of them secretly wishing they had such love in their own lives.

# 14

# Creativity, Peace and Prophecy

Morganite clapped his hands, and the crystal disappeared in an instant. He took a bow and quietly returned to his seat. Opal leapt from her chair. She was excited that her turn had come. Opal was a little wild in nature and had found it incredibly difficult to sit still for the duration of the show. She was full of energy and ready to show the audience her unique gifts. She pirouetted to the centre of the ring in a slightly uncoordinated mélange of a ballet dancer and a spinning top. Her arms were wide open and stretched to the sky, and her legs were apart. 'Good day, all! Or should I say good evening to you!' she yelled. 'It's my turn! Far out!'

• • •

She reached into her top and revealed a pencil. She walked around them holding the pencil in each of their faces. She stopped and returned to the centre. She took two steps, then passed the pencil to Sapphire, who took it. Opal then pulled a roll of paper from under the seat she had been sitting in and lay it on the floor. She asked Sapphire if she would draw a picture of Opal.

Sapphire laughed, knowing that she was downright hopeless at drawing, but Opal was insistent. Sapphire crouched on the floor, pencil in hand, and drew. It was not long before she was finished.

Opal frowned 'Seriously, Sapphire, you cannot be finished. You only just started!'

Sapphire laughed again only louder this time. 'Sorry, Opal. You picked the wrong student. I have no talent for drawing. I have the creativity of a two-year-old, and even then, they would do better.' They all laughed quietly.

Opal gave a tiny smile which did not reach the sides of her face. 'Sapphire, why don't you show the everyone the picture you have drawn.'

Sapphire rolled her eyes. 'Seriously? If you insist.' She lifted the paper up and turned it around slowly so they could all see her picture. Everyone laughed much louder this time. On the page was a simple stick man image. Sapphire looked pleased with herself. 'Well, at least it made you smile. That is the depth of my drawing talent folks. I kid you not.'

The laughter eventually stopped after some of the witches laughed so hard, they either fell off their chairs or sloshed their drinks on the ground.

'Okay, okay, settle down.' Opal said, trying to take back control. She took the pencil from Sapphire's hand and placed it in her own mouth. She drew it back from her mouth and passed it back to Sapphire.

Sapphire scrunched up her face. 'No way. You just slobbered all over that. I'm not touching it!' She leaned back further in the chair so that Opal could not touch her with the pencil.

Opal said, 'The pencil is dry, Sapphire. Humour me, please,' in a quieting tone.

Sapphire leaned forward slowly. She did not want to ruin Opal's display but was not excited by the idea of holding a pencil covered in saliva. She tentatively took the pencil from Opal. 'Okay. I have it. Now what?'

Opal was pleased she had chosen to help. 'Thank you, Sapphire. Now, please draw me.'

Sapphire rolled her eyes again and had a pained expression on her face. 'What? Again? For goodness sake, I told you, I cannot draw. Look at my picture!'

Opal picked up the stick man drawing and tore it into pieces. 'Draw, Sapphire. Please.' Sapphire began to sketch on the paper as she had before. Then, a crowd of multi-coloured butterflies appeared. They surrounded Sapphire, brushing against her face, hair, hands—all over her. Sapphire looked nervous 'What on earth?'

The crowd gasped at the array of colours on the magical creatures. They were butterflies, but nothing like the butterflies they were used to seeing in an ordinary garden. They were bright, and each one carried several different colours and markings. They were luminous against the black of the sky. Sapphire tried to draw amidst the frenzy of delicate wings around her person. She stopped drawing—almost as quickly as she had the first time.

Morganite said 'here we go again! Show some willingness, Sapphire. At least try.'

Opal smiled. She took the sheet from Sapphire. She slowly raised it to the light so that it could be seen. They were astonished at the result. There on the paper was almost a mirror image of Opal which had been sketched in charcoal by Sapphire.

Sapphire appeared dazed but was smiling now. 'Wow, I can draw,' she said.

Opal nodded. 'Yes, you can, Sapphire. Yes, you can.' The butterflies flew into the night sky, and the witches were stunned into silence. Opal returned the pencil to her pocket and sat back in her seat.

Pearl was next. She walked into the middle of the Witches carrying herself stiffly but graciously. She was not a Witch who enjoyed displays like this, but she understood the importance of their community and the combined strength of the White Witches. Pearl was not in the least shy; she was merely intolerant of public demonstrations. She had enough confidence in herself not to desire the attention. She took out a shell from her purse. She opened it and pulled out a lip gloss. She placed her finger in the lip gloss and gently dabbed her lips, then closed the shell and placed it back in her purse.

She walked over to Morganite. 'Touch up?' she asked.

Morganite always liked his make-up perfect. Therefore, Pearl knew he would not refuse her.

'Oh, yes, dear,' replied Morganite. Pearl took the shell from her purse, placed her finger in the liquid and touched Morganite's mouth, applying it on his full lips. Morganite rubbed his top and bottom lip together to ensure it had been distributed evenly. 'Thank you, dear.'

Pearl waited for a moment then asked, 'Morganite, do you like me?'

Morganite replied instantly. 'No, Pearl, you are stuck up and full of your own self-importance.'

Almost as soon as he had spoken the words, he clasped his hand over his mouth as if he hadn't meant to speak. The crowd gasped, and some sniggered.

Pearl continued 'Morganite, do you like Amber?'

Morganite began to answer immediately and without regard for his words. 'She is plain, lacks the glamour and the power of many of us, but she has a nice home and knows how to throw a party.' He looked horrified. It was as though the words fell from his mouth unfiltered.

They began to laugh. They thought this was fun, but Morganite was totally shocked by his words (even if they were his thoughts). Opal fired question after question to Morganite, some more personal than others. She was revealing some of Morganite's darkest secrets. This went on for around ten minutes. Morganite was exhausted and not enjoying it one bit.

Opal decided it might be time to stop despite the crowd being thoroughly entertained. She said, 'Morganite, would you like me to stop?'

Morganite said, 'Yes, please.' He was humbled by the whole experience.

Pearl took a tissue from her bag. 'Then remove the gloss from your lips. This is truth serum.' Morganite quickly pulled the tissue from Pearl's hand and wiped his lips vigorously. Opal smiled wryly. 'That is what vanity can do for you, Morganite.'

Morganite did not speak another word. Although Ruby had found it funny, she did feel a little sorry for Morganite. Afterwards, they all made sure to let Morganite know there were no hard feelings by refilling his drink, bringing more snacks and providing real lip gloss.

Sapphire was up next. She moved more slowly to the centre of the group. She looked as though she had lived life to the maximum, including good food and drink, which is what the other Witches liked most about her. She was larger than life and a beautiful individual inside and out. She brought great joy to all those with whom she spent time. She had a sunny disposition and life did not phase her, no matter what happened. Sapphire's gift was one of the most difficult to show in a demonstration such as this one because Sapphire's gift is that she is a prophet, meaning she has the gift of being able to see and influence the future. She could predict what an individual might do from one minute to the next, so she showed her gift by timing her display just as one of the witches had gone to the bathroom. In this case, it was Pearl.

As Pearl disappeared through the doors of the house, Sapphire said, 'When Pearl returns you will notice she looks unhappy. She will not tell you why she is sad, but it will be obvious in her face. The reason Pearl is blue is that she has lost her pearl, which she carries on her person for safety. Pearl will not want to reveal she has lost her pearl because she knows the punishment. If she is viewed as irresponsible, her stone will be reduced to mediocre powers, and she will sit in front of Queen Diamond at the White Witches Coven to re-learn her White Witches code. She would receive a punishment dictated by Queen Diamond.'

As soon as Sapphire had finished speaking, Pearl appeared. As predicted, Pearl's face showed signs of distress. This was unusual for Pearl, as she is typically calm and collected, always in control. The witches continued to talk amongst themselves. Sapphire said she would complete her demonstration in a short while, as she was feeling a little tired. She didn't want Pearl to realise she was amidst a live demonstration.

Sapphire sat next to Pearl. 'Is everything okay, Pearl?'

Pearl was not used to this one on one attention, and she did not enjoy it. 'Yes, I am. Why are you here?' she said bluntly.

Sapphire touched her hand. 'Are you sure?'

Pearl clearly did not want to engage in conversation with Sapphire. She removed her hand and changed her position in the circle. Then she reached into her purse, pulling out item after item. Lip gloss, paper, tissues, keys, potion, a mini book of spells, mints. She returned them all to her bag, then followed the ritual again three times. Unseen by Pearl, Sapphire walked to the plant pot with all the flowers (cultivated by Moonstone earlier in the evening) and gave it a gentle push. Out dropped Pearl's magic pearl. It was shimmering and sparkling in the candlelight. All the witches saw it fall but carried on their conversations as if they had not noticed. Even Sapphire pretended she had not seen it fall to the floor. She walked on as though she had been distracted by something in the house.

Pearl dropped to the floor quickly. She scooped the pearl up faster than the speed of light and returned it to her person—down her top. With a sigh of relief, she took a large drink from her goblet and glanced around from under her eyebrows at the others in the hope that nobody had noticed. She was thankful they had not and was eager to see Sapphire's display now. Her panic was over. The other witches did not let Pearl know what they had witnessed out of respect. They understood the consequences and that it was not Pearl's fault. It served as a reminder to them to look after their precious jewels and not allow them to fall into the hands of evil. Such powerful magic in the wrong hands could put themselves, this world and their realms at risk.

# 15

# Now the party is over

The visit from the White Witches really opened Ruby's eyes to a whole new universe. There was so much to learn, and she could not wait to start. Many questions raced through her mind, like when she might visit her newfound family in their magical homes. She was also feeling a little miserable and deflated that the evening had come to an end. It had been an exhilarating but exhausting evening and one she would not forget easily. She glanced at her mother.

Amber looked weary. She had put all her energy into making the night a success for her daughter, and Ruby was grateful for that. As if reading Ruby's thoughts, the witches started to leave the party. They knew it was time to let Amber and Ruby get some rest.

Jasmine yawned and stretched. Ruby listened for the final clip-clop of heels and shoes to disappear down the garden path. Ruby and Amber walked across the garden and into the backdoor. Amber collected the post box contents on her way in.

When Jasmine was sure that she was alone again, she started to perform her magical party trick. Jasmine went to work and with a swish of her long bushy white tail cleared all the tables, swept the floor and filled the bins with leftover food and drink. The garden looked as pristine as it was before the ceremony began. Jasmine felt extremely pleased with her equally important contribution to the ceremony. The thing she was most looking forward to was the looks of confused pleasure on Ruby's and Amber's faces when they eventually returned.

Jasmine only performed her magic on rare occasions, as she did not want Amber to learn of her secret magical gifts. She had sworn an oath to the head of the White Witch Coven Queen Diamond that she would not reveal her magic to Amber or Ruby. Queen Diamond had gifted the extra power to Jasmine on the day that Sylvia's and Amber's powers had been reduced after the terrible mistake with the locket. Queen Diamond was wise. She understood that Sylvia must be punished for her carelessness, but that Sylvia and Amber would still need protection from the dark forces at times in their lives. Queen Diamond could only protect them by surreptitiously bestowing some magical abilities to Princess, now Jasmine. She loved Sylvia and Amber and did not hesitate in making sure the kitty was supported with strong enough magic to keep them all safe.

After a few short moments, Amber and Ruby returned to the garden, resigned to a long night of clearing and sweeping. To their astonishment, the garden was immaculate. The rubbish was no longer there. The goblets, cauldrons and plates had all disappeared, and the floor was clean. The chairs had been returned to their original location in the house. All the witches had left, and the garden was so quiet they could hear themselves breathing.

Amber looked at Ruby and said, 'Did you...?'

Ruby shook her head. 'No, I didn't. How could I? I was upstairs with you the whole time.'

Amber was flabbergasted. 'Well, I am impressed. It looks as though the White Witches have learned some better habits. How lovely of them. I must write to them and thank them!'

Ruby agreed. 'Yes, let's do that, but not tonight. We must first go inside and rest for a moment.'

Jasmine smiled to herself. Well, as much as a cat can smile! Jasmine turned and winked at Mo Charaid, the only witness to the whole magical clearing up activity. The cat then stretched her tail high in the air with pride and sauntered back into the house following Amber and Ruby through the back door.

Amber collected some mugs from the drainer and poured in frothy dusky pink hot chocolate from the large iron pan on the stove. She knew it was Ruby's favourite night-time drink, especially as the temperature had dropped a little. Amber sat down and drew back the seat next to her own. It creaked with her weight, and the legs made a squeaking sound as they scraped across the floor. 'Come sit with me for a moment before bed.' She gestured to the chair.

Ruby responded by falling onto the seat with the finesse of a baby elephant.'

'Thank you for going to such a lot of trouble tonight,' Ruby said.

'You are most welcome, my darling girl. I had a wonderful time. We have such a unique family.'

They both laughed as they knew how bizarre the night's events would look to a regular person. 'Ruby, you only really saw a smidgeon of our gifts and our world. What is important is that you visit the homes of each Witch and see how they live. Get to know them a little better.'

Ruby was both excited and afraid of the proposal. Yes, she wanted to see this amazing new world and experience all that it had to offer, but she was reluctant to leave her mother on her own for what might be a long time.

Amber carried on. 'It would take a little time, but when you are there, time will pass so quickly. It will feel like it is all over in a blink. This is the chance of a lifetime for you, Ruby.'

Ruby recognized that it would be difficult to return to her previous life and circle of friends knowing what she now knew. Although her friends were dear to her, she knew she must learn what it meant to be part of the family into which she was born. This was her destiny.

Amber continued carefully, allowing Ruby to digest all she was proposing. She wanted Ruby to understand the importance of what she was proposing. 'You may have heard of the Queen of the White Witches Coven;

her name is Queen Diamond. Queen Diamond has reached an age in Witching years, where she can no longer serve the Witching community. White Witch rules say she can only serve as the head of the Coven for one hundred years, and then she must be replaced so a new queen can lead the Coven. A new queen who will bring with them a fresh perspective and new wisdom. In that way, the White Witches remain one step ahead of the dark side. Queen Diamond has served the White Witch Coven for almost one hundred years. As such, the Coven must find a new Queen.'

Ruby was unsure how this related to her, but she was eager to find out. Her head was filled with more questions. Why must she visit the others, and who makes the rules? What happens to the White Witch Queen when she stops serving? Ruby did not want to interrupt her mother. She remained quiet, but her thoughts had started to go in slow motion, and things were becoming hazy and muddled. She was falling asleep. She slumped in her chair with her head slightly rested on Amber's shoulder, one hand still gripped around the mug of hot chocolate. Jasmine saw this as a great opportunity. She tiptoed across the table, placed her pink nose in the mug and began to lap up the drink, purring loudly with contentment.

# 16

# The Invitations

Ruby opened one eye as a break in her bedroom curtains let a bossy stream of sunshine into her room. The sun felt warm across her pale eyelids. She opened the other eye, and as her mind started to awaken, she recalled last night's ceremony. For half a moment, she thought it might have all been a dream. She pushed her hand into the pocket of her dress to reassure herself that it was all real. She found the pouch and gripped it to reassure herself that the ruby was still there. It was not a dream; it was the reality of her new life. Her heart was pleased and full of warmth like the sun that had gently touched her face only moments earlier. It was as if it was gently trying to awaken her from her slumber.

# The Invitations

Ruby realised she had fallen asleep in her dress and quickly removed it. She pulled a clean dress from the closet. She stepped into the clean dress. It smelt like fresh flowers. Her mother used a special scent in her washing that was comforting and familiar. The dress was a large grey, sack-like dress. She liked to wear it as loungewear. She stepped into the corridor and saw her mother.

'Good morning, Ruby. Breakfast is on the table. I thought we might read through the invitations the Witches left in the post last night. Would that be okay?'

Ruby gave her mum a hug. 'Yes, please, Mother. That would be lovely.' They walked down the stairs together. The invites were all stacked neatly on the table, each in the colour of the precious jewel each witch owned. Ruby spooned the breakfast into her mouth. It was warm porridge oats. She was hungry and wanted to eat and recharge her energy levels before reading the invites from her new family. The envelopes were all shapes and sizes. There were circles, diamonds, stars and triangles. They were not your conventional envelopes—they were all made of glass. Emerald's invite was round and green, Alexandrite's was triangular and pale blue, Moonstone's was the shape of a half-moon and white, Pearl's was hexagonal and cream-coloured, Opal's was oblong and shiny black metallic, Sapphire's was a blue diamond and Morganite's was peach and flower-shaped.

Ruby opened Emerald's invitation first. Amber showed Ruby that if she tapped on the glass, the envelope would open, and the words would literally float into the air. Ruby did exactly as she was instructed, and the words started to appear in the air before her face.

Ruby read aloud. 'Welcome to the family, Ruby. I would like to cordially invite you to my space in the world. I live in White Witch Coven. I have so many things to show you. Please come soon. Love, Emerald.' She opened the invite from Alexandrite and the same thing happened. Amber told Ruby the words in the invites would only appear when read by a White Witch. The words were similar on all the invites except the destinations differed. Alexandrite and Moonstone asked Ruby to come to their home named The Moon of Validor. Pearl's invite was to Healing Island. Opal's was to Compassion Crystal Mountain. Sapphire's to Wisdom Dome and lastly, Morganite invited Ruby to Little Love Forest.

Ruby was so honoured to have received the invites from the witches, but she was sad to leave her mother, Jasmine and Mo Charaid. She knew that they would be waiting and praying for her safe return. There was a moment of silence whilst both Amber and Ruby seemed to be thinking the same thing and feeling the same sorrow. However, they both knew that this was an essential part of Ruby's White Witch training and that they should be grateful for such a unique opportunity. Amber knew it had been some time since a member of her family had been blessed with all the powers of a White Witch, and she was pleased for Ruby. She wanted to give Ruby the best chance possible to make a difference in this world and in the realm of the Validor.

# The Invitations

The strangest thing about going on a trip such as this is that as you have never been where you're going, it is difficult to know what to take with you. Ruby searched her mother's face for inspiration. Amber's face was positively calming and relaxed, which helped Ruby to stay calm and do what needed to be done.

Almost afraid to hear the response, Ruby whispered, 'When must I go?' Although they had talked at length of Validor and what Ruby must do, they had never discussed when.

Amber looked out of the window as if searching for something. 'There is only one time when you can go. The time when both gateways to the Witching world are open—when there is thunder and lightning.'

'Thunder and lightning?' Ruby exclaimed. 'You said that was God moving the furniture!.'

Amber laughed. 'You must forgive me for that. I was trying to put your mind at rest.'

Ruby did not feel she received a proper answer to her question. 'So how will I know what day that will be?'

Amber smiled. 'The Witches have the timetable for when thunder and lightning will occur. We rely on it to get around. It is a little like a bus or train timetable in this world. So, Ruby, to answer your question, the next bus is at midnight tonight.'

Ruby swallowed hard. She had not expected it to happen so soon. 'What will I need to take with me?'

Amber could hear the panic in her daughter's words. 'Everything will be okay; you will need nothing except faith that you will be looked after through the perils of this journey. Take with you the knowledge that although it will not be easy, you will be surrounded by those you love and positive energies who only want good for you. You may not always see this, but when you feel distressed, visualise it in your mind's eye.'

# 17

# Lightning Pass and Thunder Tunnel

Ruby looked at the clock. Her eyes were heavy now. She was used to being in bed long before now. The large grandfather clock had stood in the hallway for almost a century, its dark oak body tired and warped from the passage of time. It looked as though it was balancing with one clock-like foot on the floor, almost as if it were hopping. It was eleven forty-five in the evening. The rain hammered the leaded glass window as though it were threatening to come in. The wind howled like a troop of wild mountain dogs, the sound was rising and sinking in unison, seemingly rehearsed to bring an eerie and mystical feel to the evening. Ruby could no longer see the mountains through the windowpanes.

Ruby said, 'What a strange night this is. It looks as though even the mountains have disappeared.'

Amber was proud of Ruby's observation and realised that Ruby's White Witch view of the world was becoming stronger and stronger.

'That is because they have disappeared. The world has always assumed that when darkness falls, it just means we can no longer see things because the sun isn't providing any light. However, what really happens is that everything disappears. The mountains only exist in your own mind when it is dark. In the world of White Witches, when darkness falls and thunder and lightning begins, behind the darkness is not mountains and buildings; behind the darkness is the realm of Validor. If the sun were to come back to us, even for a moment, the images behind the darkness would be different from those we had seen before the sunset. Thunder and lightning are designed to be frightening to serve as a deterrent to regular people and persuade them not to go out at night. If they go out, they may learn the truth. We have all heard the stories of people being struck by lightning or falling buildings and trees during a storm. This is White Witch magic, and they do it to stop humans going out during a storm, so they don't find the gateways to the realm of Validor. The secret of the Realm of Validor must be kept hidden at all costs. If the powers of the Nine Precious Jewels were ever to fall into the wrong hands, it could lead to a path of destruction which threatens both the world as we know it and the realm of Validor.'

Amber went on to explain that the realm of Validor only has a moon which lights the sky; it does not have a sun. The moon could create light and darkness, but Ruby would learn more about this on her visit to Validor. Ruby nodded to indicate that she understood. Her new world was starting to take its place in the jigsaw puzzle she was creating in her mind. Ruby did not know what the new jigsaw of her life would look like once complete, or if it would ever be complete.

Amber rose from her favourite seat in the lounge. It was a large seat with a high back that made it look rather like a throne. She had left Ruby for the best part of the day to allow her to enjoy her home one last time before embarking on her pilgrimage. She had spent the day reading and listening to her favourite music. Amber walked to the cloakroom and took a dusty cloak from a peg. The knob was almost falling off the wall with the weight of the cloak. There were several other cloaks on the peg, but she only needed two—one for herself and one for Ruby to wear on her journey.

'I know I said you would not need to take anything with you, but there is one thing I would like you to take.' She passed the cloak to Ruby. It was black and creased but felt like velvet to touch. Inside the cloak it was silver. 'This was my mother Sylvia's cloak. Your grandmother's. I want you to wear this on your travels. Your grandmother would have been so proud that she had a grandchild like you and that she could still carry on the White Witch purpose through you.'

Ruby was not overly keen on the smell of the cloak, but she knew that this would be important to her mother and her grandmother. She threw the cloak around her shoulders so that it aligned to her frame correctly. The movement created a little dust cloud which made them both cough, but Ruby was too polite to mention that it was covered in years of dust. She struggled to find, the clasp, so Amber helped her. The clasp was silver and brooch-like with the letter "S" inscribed on the back. She tipped it to the dim light in the cloakroom to see the front. It felt like marble to the touch, and on closer examination, she could see an extremely old black and white picture with a yellow background. The photo was of a woman whose hair was piled high on her head She wore three rows of beads around her neck. Her lips were full and smiling. She was pretty.

Ruby wanted to ask who the woman was, but before she could, Amber said, 'Your grandmother.'

Amber looked to the floor as she said it and pretended to dust her own cloak, which was bronze.

Ruby realised this was an emotional moment and that her mother was finding it difficult to speak. She decided this was not the time to continue with questions about Sylvia. 'Thank you, I will cherish this.'

Amber nodded. They walked slowly to the front door. Just as they reached the door, they heard the patter of four paws in the hallway, followed by the sound of stone dragging across the floor. They turned to find Jasmine and Mo Charaid.

'Ah, Jasmine, Mo Charaid, I will miss you so much, but it is important you stay and look after mother whilst I am not here.'

They both flopped to the floor. Ambers face tensed as Jasmine had dragged Mo Charaid into the hallway with her tail and created a large scratch in the floor, but she forgave them, as she knew their intentions were good. Ruby kissed Jasmine's face lightly and gave Mo Charaid a pat on the head.

'I won't be long. You will see.' With that, Ruby opened the front door.

Amber gripped Ruby's elbow.

'I had been meaning to mention, only I did not want you to be upset. You will be quite some time. Completing your White Witch training means visiting many different realms. You will learn things that give you wisdom beyond your years. So, each time you pass through one, you will grow six months older. This way, when you return, humans will not be suspicious of your wisdom. In other words-you will leave as a child and return as a woman.'

Ruby clamped her teeth together so that her mother would not see she was upset. Leaning forward she kissed her briskly on the cheek.

'It's okay mother, I understand. Please don't worry'

• • •

The furious wind was now barging its way into the narrow hallway, nearly ripping the door out of Ruby's hand. She and Amber pulled up their hoods at the same time and stepped out of the door and into the storm.

The wind pushed on their legs which made them feel like they were walking through treacle. Their hoods blew down within seconds, and their hair was blown in all directions like the legs on an octopus.

The wind made it difficult to talk to each other, but Amber shouted as loud as she was able. 'Head for the barn!'

Ruby was confused. 'What barn?' Ruby didn't know they even had a barn. The grounds surrounding her mother's home were so vast it could be anywhere.

'Follow me,' Amber replied.

It was becoming more and more difficult to walk as they tried to push themselves through wind that felt like a wall of steel. The wind felt as if it was blowing at one hundred miles per hour, which was not unusual for the mountain location. It was just unusual to attempt to go out into such winds.

Her mother travelled to the west of the house, keeping her head down. Ruby followed. The ground was solid, but Ruby had her lace-up brown leather walking boots on which were comfortable around her feet. The rain had stopped, which was a blessing, but they both knew it would not last. The ground was still wet from the previous rain tantrum that had been thrown by mother nature. Two or three minutes of stomping passed before they reached an old farm barn. The walls were still intact, but the roof had seen better days and was sliding to one side of the building. The double wooden doors had iron castings on them and an iron bar across to keep them closed. Amber signalled to Ruby that they must remove the iron bar together. They each took a side and pushed and pulled. At first, they wiggled the iron bar to free it from its braces, and then, with a last push and heave, they freed it from its brackets. Ruby threw it to the floor. They ran into the building to shelter from the storm.

The barn was mostly empty. There were a few old cauldrons, paint pots and farm tools, plus some. sticks of straw strewn around the stone floor. In the corner, there was something beneath a large grey canvas cloth. Ruby pulled it off in one quick movement. It was an old pale blue, rickety Ford pickup truck. Ruby guessed it had been there for at least fifty years. Her heart sank. She could not believe her mother expected them to travel in such an unreliable, old vehicle in extreme conditions.

'This was my first car, Ruby. My trusty old steed. It has never let me down. It will keep us safe; I promise.' Ruby was not so confident, but she sort of admired the fact that her mother was not like the other witches. She was not flashy and ostentatious, or a showoff; she was a humble and simple lady with a good heart.

'Well, okay. If you are sure,'

They pulled at the door handles and the paint crumbled into their hands. The doors creaked open, falling a little as they did. They scrambled into the worn leather seats. Amber looked perplexed. 'Er I don't have the keys, Ruby. So sorry. Would you run back to the house to get them?'

Ruby could not believe her mother had been so disorganised, and she was dreading the walk back to the house. The conditions were horrendous, and she was not sure she would make it. She sighed and was about to get back out of the car when Amber said,

91

'Ha-ha. I'm just kidding, Ruby. This car does not need a key or petrol, but it was fun to see the look on your face.' They both laughed.

Amber clicked her fingers and the car jerked to life. It started to buck like a horse as it tried to balance itself. Ruby realised they had started to rise into the air and could see the floor of the barn a short distance below. This was magical. The headlights had turned on, so the path outside the door was clearly visible. 'Ready?' Amber said.

'Ready!'

The car rose into the air to the height of the barn doors. It paused, almost as if it didn't want to go out into the storm. Then, with a swift push forward, it launched itself into the night sky. Amber tried to keep the car low so as not to bring attention to it. Too often White Witches had been mistaken for UFOs, and it created no end of unsolved mystery television. Although those stories always gave the White Witches a little giggle, it was not advised. The wind battled with the car, but it was a losing battle; the car was powered by magic!

The heavens opened. It was like the contents of a hundred swimming pools crashing onto the roof of the car. It shook the car and made Amber and Ruby jump out of their seats, but it did not stop the wonderful old car from pushing on.

'Like I said, my trusty steed. His name is Rust Bucket Man.'

Ruby laughed. 'Seriously, mother? Rust Bucket Man?'

Amber laughed. 'Yes, Rust Bucket Man. When I first realised he could fly, I said to my mother, "He is

92

like Rust Bucket Man." My mother said, "He is Rust Bucket Man." So, it's kind of stuck.'

'Hmm, maybe he should be called something else really.' Ruby teased. Amber put her fingers to her lips

'Shh, he likes his name. Do not offend him.'

Ruby was not sure if her mother was serious but did not carry on the conversation, just in case. They needed to get to the gateway after all.

What was most amazing was that when they passed over villages and towns, there were scarcely any people on the streets and those that were had umbrellas or raincoats and were so preoccupied with getting to their destination that they did not notice Rust Bucket Man. It occurred to Ruby that she didn't have any idea where they were going. 'Do you know the way,?' she asked.

Amber nodded. 'Rust Bucket Man knows the way.' They were flying across fields and forests at a rapid pace. The speed was quite disorientating, and Ruby started to feel sick. They ground to a halt. The car had become entangled in the trees. It began wriggling and writhing to get away.

Ruby said, 'Oh, no! What can we do?' The more the car struggled, the tighter the sinewy branches gripped. The car stopped moving, and Ruby heard someone speak.

'Okay, you win. Just let me go. It is not funny any-more.' The voice seemed to come from the car. Ruby turned her head furiously but could not see anyone else.

'When will you learn whose boss, Rust Bucket Man?' a silky feminine voice responded. 'It is getting dull; you do this every time, Teressa.'

Ruby realised the car was talking, and it was talking to the tree.

Amber joined the discussion. 'Enough is enough, children. You have had your fun. Let us be on our way.'

Teressa replied, 'Only when he says I am the best.'

There was a short silence, and the car seemed to deflate as if in protest. Then his engine roared back to life. 'Fine. You are the best, Teressa. Now, let us go!'

The tree slid its branches away, allowing the car to take flight. Amber looked at Ruby. 'This is just the start of it, my girl. Life will never be the same again. Before my mother lost all her powers, she found it entertaining to make trees more humanlike. Teressa was one of them, but there are many more scattered around this world and Validor. They used to be my mother's watch guards if you will.'

Ruby was both amazed and proud of her grandmother's clever thinking. 'I guess even a White Witch cannot be everywhere,' Ruby said.

'Indeed, sometimes our trees provide early warning of potential threats or unwanted visitors,' replied Amber.

They had been floating for some time, and Ruby was ever curious. 'How do we get to Validor?'

Amber pointed to the sky. 'There are two gateways. One is named Thunder Pass and the other Lightning Pass.'

Ruby listened to her mother's explanation of the gateways especially carefully, as she knew this was the only allowed connection to Validor. She realised her grandmother had taken an unauthorised route to Pixie Land. Pixies could not travel outside of their land using Lightning Pass and Thunder Tunnel. Pixie Land was also in Validor, but it was surrounded by a wall of magic, which meant if a Pixie wanted to visit any other part of Validor, they would first need to use their usual gateway via a picture, then find Thunder Tunnel or Lightning Pass. White and Sable Witches preferred to keep the meddling Pixies at arm's length; they had enough trouble keeping the peace amongst themselves. The same did not apply to the fairies, however. Fairies also lived in Validor in Fairy Gardens, but they were a peaceful and good bunch who generally kept to themselves.

Ruby learned that Lightning Pass was the White Witch gateway and Thunder Tunnel was the Sable Witch gateway. Each passageway was a totally different travel experience. A new Witch must cross areas during her formative pilgrimage, which was how the "Alliance Gateway Agreement" between Sable and White Witches arose. It was one of the few agreements to which both the Sable and White Witches adhered. The reason they were able to agree this was that the White Witches thought it built strength, while the Sable Witches saw it as a way to have fun with new White Witches. The White Witches, however, realised that the arrangement worked both ways. Just as the Sable Witches were learning White Witch magic, the White Witches were also learning sable magic. It was of benefit for both Covens; thus, the agreement was struck by a wise council of Witches that met for important decisions and the setting of law between the two Covens.

Ruby asked what would happen if either Coven chose to use a gateway that was not their own. Amber explained this would have serious consequences, as it could mean that either a sable became a white, a white become sable, or that they would stay as they are but remain a prisoner in the opposite realm.

'So how can we reach the gateway,?' Ruby asked.

'Lightning Pass can only be entered at the fork of the lightning bolt as it strikes. Thunder Tunnel is directly next door to this but can only be entered when a clap of thunder occurs, and the gateway opens.'

Amber started to steer the car to the ground, gradually and gently. She was relieved to have reached the foot of Lightning Pass.

'Rust Bucket Man, thank you, we will make our own way from here. Please go home and be safe,' said Amber. It was only at this point that Ruby noticed that Rust Bucket Man had a uniquely comical face, with big eyes (headlamps) surrounded by eyelashes and a big cheeky grin. Rust Bucket Man could not go beyond this point, and the remainder of the journey must be on foot because the car was not a witch, and the rules were that nothing or nobody, but witches must approach the gateway or know of its location.

'This is where we are on our own,' Amber said. 'Grab your cloak, we must walk the remaining distance. Ruby knew not to argue and was glad for the walk. Every part of her body ached as she had been crammed into the confined space of the car for what felt like hours. She stepped out of the car, stretching and bending as she stood. Amber hurried her along, wrapping her coat firmly around Ruby's shoulders as the rain started to pour. 'Hurry, we do not have long.'

They started to walk quickly, then broke into a run. The rain streamed down their faces and into their eyes, noses and mouths. Their capes whipped around their legs. The rain on their faces was starting to turn to ice and made their vision blurry. Ruby thought, *why would the Witches pick such an uncomfortable way to move across the realms?*

'Isn't there an easier way,?' she asked.

'No, none, I am afraid. This route was created before prehistoric times and has worked successfully since then.'

Just as Ruby had started to feel despondent, she saw the lightning strike right before them. The brightness of the it hurt their eyes and lit up the whole area. The air was hot and like a furnace drying their faces and clothes in nano seconds. Just as the lightning appeared a crack of thunder rippled across the sky. It was so loud they could not hear each other even if they shouted.

Amber pointed to the left of the lightning fork. Ruby shaded her eyes to see. A large swirling circle of red mist was visible. It looked like a red cinnamon pastry swirl, only much larger and extremely foreboding. She knew she must be hungry to make that comparison. She rushed at the swirling ball of smoke as fast as she could. She was not the best runner but knew today she must do her best. She kept running, tripping on stones rolling under her feet and twisting her ankles. When the wind approached her from the opposite direction, she would inadvertently step on her cloak, which would give her shoulder a jolt and send shooting pain down her back. She was determined to keep running, but the rain itself felt like marbles being thrown in her face at point-blank range. She was nearly there; she was going to make it!

Then she fell to the ground, crashing onto some tree roots in her path. As she fell, she glanced back to try to comprehend why she had fallen. Her cloak was tangled on something. She rubbed her eyes and realised the thing that had caught her coat was her mother!

Amber shouted out, 'Wrong gateway,' then released Ruby's cloak once she was convinced Ruby would go no further. She was exhausted. Ruby could run faster than her and was so much younger. Her face was filled with panic. They only had seconds to reach Lightning Pass. 'Look to the right!'

Ruby spun her head to the right and there it was. It was like the fork of the lightning was growing wide into a triangle shape in front of her eyes. The brightness of the light emanating from the triangle was excruciating but also hypnotic. For a moment she thought she could see large brilliant white angel-like hands reaching out from the triangle, beckoning her to come closer. She looked back at her mother as she drew near to the angel hands. Knowing this would be the last time she would see her for many years. She wanted confirmation that this was the right gateway.

Her mother looked heartbroken but urged her on, swishing her hand back and forth in the direction of the gateway. Amber was still on her hands, and knees on the floor, desperately trying to catch her breath. 'Go on, I will see you soon, I promise.'

At that moment, Ruby felt her heart might break. She did not know if she would ever see her mother again. 'I can't go, Mother! What if I don't see you again?' Ruby began to cry.

Amber knew she must convince Ruby to make the leap. She crawled closer to her, dragged herself off the floor into standing position whilst being pushed in every direction by the storm. 'I would not let you go if I thought that was true. Have faith. You will see me again soon. We have no time. You must go!'

Ruby was wiping the tears from her face, and her chest felt heavy with sorrow. 'I love you,' she shouted through the tears.

'I love you, too, Ruby.' With that, Ruby stepped into the triangle. The storm silenced. Amber brushed the tears from her own cheeks. She wanted to stay strong for Ruby It was up to Ruby now. She had prepared her daughter as much as she was able, and she must now wait for the next time she would see her.

Hands reached out to Ruby and pulled her safely from the light-filled channel of energy. She found herself floating slowly on air. Her eyes brimmed with tears that eventually trickled down her face. She desperately fought to ignore the pain in her chest that had grown since she left her mother. Her dress began to unravel like it was a long length of cotton on a bobbin. Ruby was a little concerned that she would be left in only underwear. There had been no mention of losing your clothes in the tunnel! As she was wondering how to avoid extreme embarrassment, she saw a large piece of thick white ribbon floating towards her like silk waving in the breeze. It started to wrap itself around her from the waist up, then the waist down. It was quite relaxing, almost like being dusted by a thousand feathers all at once.

She ran her hands over her new dress created by the ribbon. It was white lace with a Victorian look to it. It had a fitted top and a box neckline trimmed with red lace. The skirt was bell-shaped, and the sleeves of the dress were snug the top of her arm and fluted at the bottom. She felt like a Princess.

Ruby continued to float effortlessly down the mass beam of light in her new attire. She was a passenger on the river of air, and her destination was in, well, someone else's hands. She noticed a loosely fitted red sash around her waist. On the edge of it, she could read the words "Student White Witch." Her hair had dried, and she looked angelic floating weightlessly on the air. After what felt like an hour, Ruby saw an exit. It was triangle-shaped but appeared to be swaying and bending, changing shape from time to time. She reached the exit but became stuck in what felt like sticky thread. She was motionless at the mouth of the channel. She had no clue what to do next; this pilgrimage had not come with instructions.

All Ruby did know was that she was tired and hungry. She had been awake all night and combined with the physical and emotional rollercoaster she had just experienced, it was no surprise that she began to fall asleep. As she drifted off into dream space, thousands of tiny golden-coloured creatures crawled out of the vortex walls. They were the same creatures—gold thread beetles—who had created the web of golden thread where Ruby now lay suspended. They were minuscule, smaller than ants. The thread beetles set to work. They began cleaning Ruby and untangling her hair. Others poured a golden syrup into Ruby's mouth. The syrup was a food and drink substitute, and it would revive and refresh Ruby preparing her for her adventures in Validor. Ruby slept and slept.

# 18

# Hope Coast

When the beetles were sure Ruby had rested enough, they started to remove her from the web. They made sure every thread was removed and untraceable. They often recycled the thread as they were all for saving the planet and not making Validor an unclean place to live. The beetles started to queue in uniformed lines until there were so many lines it seemed to be at least a mile long and a mile wide. Hundreds of golden beetles created a blanket of gold stretching as far as the eye could see. A cluster of them broke away and started to shuffle underneath Ruby, who was laid out on the marble floor and still fast asleep. Then with all the strength they had, they lifted Ruby and carried her above their heads. Upon reaching the larger unit, the beetles passed her across their heads until she was in the centre of the golden blanket.

One of the beetles at the front of the blanket stepped forward to face the troops. 'Okay, men, I am your drill sergeant today. Follow my orders, just like we trained, and you will not go wrong. Now, repeat after me. I don't know what she has done, should have stayed at home with Mum. Sable Witches here, Sable Witches there, they will boil her blood and chop her hair. Beetles here to save the day, keep Ruby safe and on her way.'

The beetles began a slow and laborious march toward a wonderfully ornate umbrella. The stick of the umbrella was firmly jammed into sand, and the umbrella seemed to have several tiers, all in different colours with ribbons dangling delicately from each of its supporting metal prongs. The beetles knew if they could keep Ruby beneath the umbrella, all would be well. They carefully crouched down as if performing a dance, foot by foot, leg by leg, they knelt on the floor. It took a little longer than usual, as the beetles had 12 legs each. On each foot was a lace-up boot. Once the beetles had Ruby safely on the ground, their mission was complete.

The drill sergeant turned to face his soldiers. 'Men, you should be proud of what you have achieved today. You are men of honour. Now, get your tiny butts back to Lightning Pass?'

The beetles did not need this order repeated. They ran as quickly as possible back in the direction of Lightning Pass. Some of the smaller younger beetles were struggling to keep up, so the older beetles dragged them along. It was comical to watch and quite noisy. It was surprising that Ruby did not wake instantly. Unbeknown to the beetles a Sable Witch was skulking around them. She was tip toeing in the shadow of the trees in a desperate attempt not to be seen. Breathing heavily as she did in anticipation of the harm she wished to cause Ruby. Her clothes smelling of the stale sweat from a night sleeping outdoors. She had laid patiently in wait on a bed of now crushed palm tree leaves until the moment arrived when she could pounce on Ruby.

The Sable Witch was named Grenadine. She was a tall, portly female, around six feet in height. She walked with poise and grace, not unlike that of a ballerina and wore a shiny green and black ancient kimono. Her black hair was long and scraped up into a tight ball on top of her head. In the centre of her hair was a white stripe. Her friends called her skunk. Grenadine did not like the nickname as she thought it unfeminine and not sophisticated enough for the person she felt she was. She knew the nickname was an insult to her hairstyle but was not prepared to be bullied into relinquishing her individuality.

It was usually bad news if Grenadine was around. Grenadine was most renowned for her expertise with all types of magic poisons. She was respected and feared, manipulative and sneaky and as Ruby was a White Witch this made her automatically the enemy.

There were orchards surrounding the umbrella under which Ruby slept filled with plump and delicious looking citrus fruits—oranges, lemons, limes, tangerines and grapefruit. The orchard had been planted many years earlier to provide food and sustenance to visitors. Most visitors found their way to the umbrella, as it was known to be a safe retreat from any dangers. If visitors were under the umbrella, nothing would harm them. The umbrella had special powers and beneath its brightly coloured canopy grew beautiful Lotus flowers floating in a glittering pond. Most importantly, though, the umbrella was surrounded by an impenetrable White Witch forcefield.

Ruby opened her eyes and looked around. She felt refreshed yet anxious. Her surroundings were totally unfamiliar, and her last memory was being in Lightning Pass and floating towards a golden web-like door. She told herself that things might not make sense for a short while and that it was probably a waste of time trying to understand. It would be probably be like nothing she had experienced previously. She could just make out a white signpost in the distance. It was a little camouflaged by the sun. It read, Hope Coast.

Ruby was awestruck by the heart-stopping beauty around her. The sun was shining, and the air was clean and warm. She was sitting under a large umbrella which was all the colours of a rainbow. The Validor moon in its sun phase lit up each colour. Ruby was seated on the white sand. There was a pond full of pink sparkling water. It looked like fizzy pink lemonade. She tiptoed across to the pond and placed her hands in the water. Cupping them together, she collected a teacup-sized pool of liquid and held it to her mouth, tipping it in slowly as she was unsure of its flavour. It tasted exactly like pink lemonade!

Floating in the pool were pink flowers, nearly the size of her hand. Their petals pointed to the sun, but the whole head of the flower was open. Ruby could see that outside the umbrella was an orchard filled with the most delicious-looking fruit. She was so grateful she had come to be in such bountiful surroundings. She sat for a while drinking in the whole experience—and more pink lemonade.!

Grenadine was feeling pleased with herself. She could see the new White Witch Ruby from where she was standing. She needed to be careful that Ruby did not see her and stayed in the shadows surrounded by trees. She had heard of Ruby; the Sable Witches had recently met at Sable Witch Coven, and Ruby had been mentioned. The Sable Witch King, Organza, announced that a "new starter" would visit Validor. They did not know exactly who she was or when she would arrive. A White Witch could choose any time from the Thunder Tunnel and Lightning Pass timetable. Imagine Grenadine's excitement when she realised she had accidentally stumbled on Ruby. She knew if she could find a way to harm Ruby, she would be rewarded by King Organza and her peers would praise her. She set to work on an evil poison. She drew several different shaped leaves from her pocket and began to crumble them in her hands by rubbing them together vigorously. They quickly become a powder. She then spat into her hand to create a runny paste. Grenadine reached into the tree and picked an orange, which she pierced with her black painted nails. Then she pushed some of the poison into each indentation made by her nails. Once she was satisfied that the juice had been absorbed into the luscious-looking orange, she rolled it towards the umbrella.

Ruby could not bear the thought of leaving the place. It was such a comforting and serene setting. She heard a thud next to her feet and noticed an orange had dropped from a tree and rolled to the umbrella. It was just outside of the canopy, but she stretched her foot and rolled the orange toward her hand. She picked it up and began to peel it. She could not wait to taste it. She wondered if it would taste anything like the oranges at home. Ruby took a large bite, then another, then another. The orange was heavenly sweet and juicy, and it melted in her mouth. She crammed in every piece, determined to enjoy it all, as it might be some time until she ate again or had a chance to taste something different.

Grenadine covered her mouth as she was sure she would cackle aloud with pleasure at what she had achieved. It was not long until Ruby started to feel sleepy. The poison had reached her bloodstream, and she started to fall into a coma-like sleep. Grenadine's poison was designed for just this purpose. Ruby had been sitting upright on the sand, but she had now flopped to the floor. Most of her body remained under the umbrella, but the foot she had used to reach the orange was now slightly outside the canopy, and that was just the invitation Grenadine had wanted. She could not harm Ruby if she were beneath the canopy, but her foot was now accessible.

Grenadine made her way to the umbrella and reached for Ruby's foot. She gripped it with her hand and dragged Ruby from beneath the umbrella. She was unsure what to do next but did not want the burden of carrying Ruby too far, so she decided the best thing to do was to lock her inside a large tree and leave her to die. She would just slowly slip away, never to be found again. Grenadine found a tree with a wide enough girth to allow Ruby to be laid out inside it. Using her knife-like nails, she carved a doorway into the tree, scooped out the amber, then rolled Ruby inside its gooey empty trunk. She then placed the doorway back into position and sealed it with amber sap that had spilt onto the sand from the tree. Her work was complete, or at least that is what she thought for a fleeting moment until she felt a hand on her shoulder.

It was White Witch Morganite. Unlike the Sable Witches, the White Witches knew exactly what time Ruby would arrive and where to find her when she did. Morganite was a little late to arrive (as was typical of Morganite who liked to be fashionably late).

'Grenadine. Why am I not surprised?' Morganite said through gritted teeth. Grenadine was furious that her plan had been uncovered. She was desperate for recognition from King Organza and was not prepared to quit now. She just needed to think of an alternative plan and quickly. Perhaps she could kill Morganite?

'You have been busy, Grenadine. I would not have expected anything less. The only mistake you made was not anticipating the arrival of one of the White Witches. So sloppy. Tut, tut. Well, it is not your only mistake. The other mistake is that ghastly kimono combined with an archaic hairstyle and,' he lifted Grenadine's hand and held it to the light.

'Black nails. So last season's colours!'

Grenadines face tensed at the insult. In retaliation, she slapped Morganite lightly across the face.

Morganite scoffed. 'Really? Please, step aside. You don't have the strength or intellect to outmaneuver me—or the fashion sense!'

Grenadine became furious but did not want to get her newly painted nails dirty and would not stoop to what would end up being a playground brawl. She gave Morganite a little shove in protest but nothing more.

Morganite looked at the shoulder Grenadine had pushed, then dusted it as though something unpleasant was on it. He set to work reopening the tree while Grenadine watched. Morganite did have a point. He looked uniquely chic in a black high neck tunic trimmed in gold. A large leather belt, black loose fitted pants tucked into a pair of high lace-up boots and a musketeer-like hat finished the ensemble. Clothing styles in Validor were unique. Nothing was off-limits, but in the main, Witches liked the traditional gothic style. Morganite and Grenadine were exceptions to the rule.

Morganite peeled open the makeshift door still covered in liquid amber. He found Ruby asleep inside. He had been worried the tree amber might have made things much worse for her if she had as she swallowed some or drowned. Especially if large amounts had fallen from the top of the tree. Instead, the amber had fallen around her, leaving a strange space between the amber and her body. It was almost as if someone had drawn an outline around her, for the amber had not touched her skin. It was only when he saw the outline that he realised what had happened.

'Grenadine, next time, you must do your homework. Ruby's mother is named Amber. Her precious jewel is Amber. There is no way Ruby can be harmed by amber from a tree. It's basic White Witch science. Ruby is genetically protected from it. Morganite pushed the base of his hand into Grenadine's forehead. 'Now step out of my way while I try and correct the damage you have done.'

Grenadine thought about retaliation, but she knew her own magic was inferior to Morganite's. She decided it best not to pursue either of them any further. Grenadine was cowardly and not the brightest of the Sable Witches. She ran her hands over her hair, smoothed down her kimono and started to walk away. Morganite had his back to Grenadine.

'Where are you going? You will be staying with us until I say different. You will help to ensure Ruby recovers.' He turned around and looked Grenadine in the eye in a threatening manner. 'Do you have a problem with this Grenadine?'

Grenadine looked at the floor as if focused on her shoes. 'I suppose not,' she replied.

'Good, help me to carry Ruby into the umbrella.'

Grenadine was confused. 'I cannot go under the umbrella. Everyone knows that.'

Morganite now had Amber in his arms. She looked like a rag doll, limp and lifeless.

'Yes, you can. You just cannot harm anyone whilst you are in there.' They walked to the umbrella and climbed under. Morganite gently placed Ruby on the ground as if he was afraid of breaking her. He was still consumed with anger at Grenadine but did not want to waste further energy or time on her. He needed to act quickly if he was to stop the poison from reaching Ruby's heart.

Morganite moved over so that he was at the foot of the pond. It was now clear in colour. The pond water was magical; it would change into whatever liquid someone wanted or needed. Ruby had thought of pink lemonade, but Morganite needed water. He took two pink Lotus flowers from the pond and began to chant unusual sounds. He returned them to the water and held them submerged. When he lifted them out once again, they filled with water. He shuffled over to Ruby and held the flowers over her so that the water dropped on each part of her body. He was careful to ensure all her body had been touched by the water from the pond. Still chanting loudly in a peculiar way, he brushed her face with the Lotus, making sure not to hurt her or the flower. This went on for some time. Darkness fell, and the golden thread beetles returned to the umbrella providing light for the ongoing ceremony. They had formed a semi-circle around the canopy, shimmering in the darkness.

Eventually, Morganite stopped chanting. Sweat was pouring off his face as he seemed to be absorbing the toxin from Ruby. Grenadine stayed quiet the whole time contemplating the evening's events. She occasionally nodded off but was desperately trying to stay awake as she did not trust Morganite. If she had taken advantage of Ruby in her sleep, someone might think to do the same to him. The temperature dropped on the beach as the moon of Validor had completed its cycle of light and dropped into its darkness cycle.

Morganite placed the Lotus back into the pond. He thanked the flowers for their help and then clapped his hands in the air. His hands held a golden ball of light which he carefully placed on the ground. It was a ball of fire that provided heat throughout the area under the umbrella. He noticed Grenadine kept drifting off then jumping as though reminding herself she must not sleep.

'Go to sleep, Grenadine. I told you, no one is harmed under this umbrella. The umbrella is a refuge for all who sit beneath it, even Sable Witches.' Grenadine slapped her head as if chastising herself, then lay down in the sand in a temper, tossing this way and that until eventually she was asleep.

When Morganite was sure Grenadine was asleep, he stepped out of the umbrella and pulled his pink Morganite stone from his pocket. He pointed the stone to the stars and created a message. He wanted to let the Witches know that all was not well with Ruby but that she was hopefully on the road to recovery. He left the message in the stars through the night just to ensure the White Witches had a chance to read it. Although the message was visible in the night sky, the Sable Witches could not read it because it was written in special White Witch code.

The moon of Validor returned to its sun phase. Validor had no sun and one moon, so the moon simply turned through the day from light to dark. What this meant is that when it was dark in Validor, it was darker than anything you've experienced on earth. Morganite awoke first and put the fire out by clapping around it twice.

The sound of clapping caused Grenadine to stir and the beetles to scurry away. Morganite checked on Ruby. She was still asleep. Morganite did not know what to do. He had tried his best most of the night to extract the poison using the Lotus. He could only think to go through the whole ritual again, but this time he would need Grenadine's help. He asked her to join him next to Ruby and copy exactly everything he did.

'I'm not entirely comfortable helping with a White Witch spell. What if it gets back to Organza?'

Morganite sighed. 'Organza will not find out, Grenadine. Your secret is safe with me. If you do not tell the White Witches I showed, you the ceremony. I will not tell the Sable Witches you helped. What goes on tour stays on tour?'

Morganite offered his hand to Grenadine to shake. Grenadine accepted it but let go quickly. She wanted to emphasise her reluctance to take part.

'Okay let's do this,' Morganite said. Grenadine followed Morganite's actions and chants as best she could, hitting a few wrong keys sometimes, which made Morganite scowl at her. The thread beetles reappeared and started to climb over Ruby's body, covering her from head to toe. It was like a moving sea of gold rippling in the light. Then as quickly as they appeared, they disappeared.

Grenadine was the first to quit. 'Okay, enough. I am too tired, and I need to eat!.'

Morganite sat back, placing his head in his hands. What would he say to Amber? He had been so sure he could fix this. He started to feel angry again. He picked up a pebble from the sand and threw it at Grenadine 'This is all your fault!'

The stone did not hit Grenadine. She was still under the umbrella, so was protected, but the stone landed gracefully on Ruby's hand. Then her fingers started to move.

Both Witches scrambled over to her to check if they were imagining things. Sure, enough Ruby's fingers were moving, then her arms and her legs. At last, her eyes opened. Grenadine rushed forward and kissed Ruby. She was so tired she could not face more white magic ceremonies.

Ruby was totally confused. She did know who Grenadine was but was reassured to see Morganite close by. 'Morganite, what happened?'

Morganite shrugged. 'Nothing much. Great to see you, Ruby. Welcome to Hope Coast! This is Sable Witch Grenadine. She will be joining us for a short while to help you on your journey.'

Ruby looked at Grenadine. This was not how she thought things would work.

'Why would a Sable Witch help a White Witch?' She did not remember her mother mentioning that! 'If Sable Witches help White Witches, then why were they not at the White Witches Sept showing me their powers.'

Morganite smiled 'It is a long story, Ruby; we do not have time for it now. Just know that Sable Witch Grenadine will help you find your way to the Dream Cloud.'

'Will you join us, Morganite?'

'Not this time, my dear, but rest assured Grenadine is willing to help, aren't you, Grenadine?'

Once again, Grenadine looked at the ground. 'I suppose,' she said under her breath.

Ruby and Grenadine stood up. Morganite gave Ruby a hug and pointed her shoulders in the direction of travel she should take. 'Good luck, Ruby,' he said.

'Thank you, Morganite,' Ruby said enthusiastically. Ruby strode ahead, and Grenadine took tiny steps behind. Her kimono was restricting the size of her stride, and she was finding it difficult to walk.

'Can you slow down, please? I am struggling to walk in this kimono, and I am not the fittest of people,' Grenadine complained.

Ruby was full of the joys of spring and forged on with her journey. She was on a mission and no one could stop her, especially not a Sable Witch. She heard Grenadine stumble behind her. She had tripped on her kimono and stepped sideways in an uncontrollable manner. They were at the highest point of the cliff edge. Grenadine knew she was about to fall and took this as an opportunity for more wickedness. *If I fell, so would Ruby she thought.* She grabbed Ruby and hugged her tightly with both arms as they both toppled over the cliff edge. They began to summersault through the air. There was nothing they could do except pray they reached the bottom in one piece. Ruby's heart was racing, and she started to panic, wondering if she would ever see her mother again. Images of their last cosy fireside chat and their hot chocolate sprang to her mind.

Grenadine was also spinning through the air. She was now shouting for help, but there was no one to be seen, and Ruby was dizzy from trying to focus on anything. They passed each crag in the rock face in quick succession, narrowly missing all of them. The whole drop had only been a minute long, but it seemed like an eternity before they reached the bottom.

They landed softly into what seemed like warm clay surrounded by rock faces. It was dark, but Ruby could see a waterfall running down one of the rock faces. Grenadine was coughing and spluttering as she had accidentally swallowed some clay on her crash landing. The sound of her coughs echoing across the rock face walls. Ruby had no clue of where they had landed.

'Wouldn't you think they would at least have provided a map?'

Grenadine did not respond. She was too busy clawing the clay out of her mouth with both hands.

# 19

# Rat Pits and the Rat Council

The only thing Ruby felt grateful for is that they appeared to be suspended in this clay-like substance and were not sinking deeper into it.

'Are you okay, Grenadine?' Grenadine nodded as her mouth was still dry from the clay and clay dust. Ruby looked around. They were in a pit full of clay surrounded by a circular stone wall. Above them was the cliff, but they could no longer see it. They could only see daylight and the sky, which was a murky grey colour.

The clay was so thick it was impossible to move freely. They were tightly jammed into it and were struggling to breathe. Ruby gasped for breath-trying to fill her lungs with enough air to stop her from passing out. She felt as though a hippopotamus was sitting on top of her. It was funny she should think of hippopotami at that exact moment because as soon as she had the thought, a hippopotamus head emerged from the water, spraying clay all over Grenadine through its nostrils. Before Grenadine had the chance to yell, another appeared, then two more. They were surrounded by hippos, and things were getting a little cosy in the clay pond.

Grenadine was exasperated. 'Why, why me? It is always me!' She began the horrid task of removing all the clay from her face and mouth. Ruby was less concerned about the clay but more concerned that the hippos might be hungry. However, the hippos did not seem to notice that Ruby and Grenadine were in the pit. They moved slowly around the clay pond minding their own business.

Ruby wondered if she were to climb on top of a hippo and scale the wall could she reach the top? She could not think of an alternative plan, so she decided it was worth a try. She dragged one leg out of the clay with both arms and rested on the surface. She waited for one of the hippos to get close then pulled herself up onto its back backwards. The hippo did not move. She managed to sit upright on its back, then she stood up, trying to balance as best she could. She had learned gymnastics at school, and balance was one of her strengths.

Grenadine watched, then decided she would try too. However, seconds later, she failed miserably, falling headfirst back into the clay.

Ruby was still on her feet and on the hippo's back. She placed one leg on the wall and gripped a large lump of rock on the rock face to steady her. She grabbed another with the other hand. When she felt secure, she pulled the other leg up away from the hippo. She was almost there, but her hands began to slip because they were covered in clay, and it was impossible to get a firm grip on the wall. There were enough rock ledges jutting out from the walls that she could probably climb, but the clay was too slimy and slippery, and it was futile.

She returned to the hippos back for a moment; it was a better place to be than in the mud. Grenadine wanted to join her but decided it was not worth the effort. Ruby considered other ways to escape, but she was running out of ideas. From where she was sitting, it looked like they were inside a large empty volcano full of clay. There were few ways to escape if any.

'Hello? Is anyone here?' Ruby shouted. The sound of her words ricocheted off the grey and rust-coloured walls. There was no response. 'Hello?' she shouted again. Then a few moments later, the walls surrounding them started to shake. Ruby thought it was an earthquake, but once again the hippos did not seem the least bit interested. She looked up and could see a crack forming down the wall. It started as a hairline crack and then grew wider. She was sure if she could reach it, she could squeeze through.

A large shadow appeared through the crack. It was the size of a person but not person shaped. It was rat-shaped, and the rat was standing on its hind legs. Its fur was like black velvet and its eyes blue. As the walls had separated, a platform appeared from one of the walls and the rat stepped onto it. Ruby noticed an offensive smell had arrived around the same time as the rat. Shortly after, another rat stepped through the crack. Then, another one tried to do the same but became jammed in the wall due to the size of his tummy. The two rats that had made it through the crack found this funny, and they began laughing and sniggering. After three more attempts, the third rat squeezed through the crack and made it to the ledge.

'Hi,' Ruby stammered. 'Can you speak? Can you understand me?'

The first rat stepped forward. 'Indeed' he said, in a rather well-spoken English accent. 'My name is Triston, this is Augustus, and this is Gumbert. We are the Rat Council.' He smacked each of the other rats over the head as he introduced them. They tried unsuccessfully to duck and then smacked him back. 'It seems you have stumbled into Rat Pit. Who are you?'

Ruby was pleased they could understand her but was not sure if they were friendly rats or the type of rat that might want to bite or eat you. 'I am White Witch Ruby, and this is...'

Before she could finish, Triston finished the sentence for her. 'That is Sable Witch Grenadine. We know who that is. We just cannot understand why a Sable Witch and White Witch would be together. Normally, we would help a Sable Witch, as she is on the dark side, like us, but in this case, we cannot be sure of her loyalty.'

Grenadine started to protest. 'But, but,'

'No buts,' Triston said. 'We are the Rat Council. We will contact the Sable Witch Coven to determine if you can be trusted. After that, we may or may not release you.' He pulled out a notebook from a shelf on the wall and started to rifle through the pages. 'As for you, White Witch Ruby. You are not in our White Witch listings.'

Ruby nodded. 'Yes, I am a new White Witch. I am the daughter of Amber the White Witch.'

They all broke into a fit of laughter. Then Triston regained his composure. 'Oh, you must be so proud, your mother the incompetent half White Witch,' he said sarcastically. 'For a moment there, I thought we might have stumbled across someone important. Come on, council. Let's go to dinner.'

They all turned on their heels and were about to go back through the crack in the wall.

'No, wait,' Ruby said. 'Please, you cannot leave us here. I am sure we could be useful for something. I mean, perhaps we could help with dinner or something.'

Grenadine snorted. 'Maybe you can, but I am not ruining these nails for anyone.'

Ruby turned to look at Grenadine and muttered under her breath, 'If you want out of here, you will play along!'

The rats stopped in their tracks. Augustus spoke first. 'We could use them to help with the masquerade tonight. It will be busy, and they will be quicker than our usual serving staff as they have hands and feet.'

Triston looked impressed. 'That is not a bad idea, Augustus.'

Gumbert joined in. 'Sounds good to me.'

Then once again, the rats turned on their heels and started towards the doorway.

'Wait,' Ruby shouted. 'How will we get out?'

Augustus shouted back over his shoulder. 'Up the ladder, of course.'

Now Ruby was totally flummoxed. *What ladder?* Just as she had queried its existence in her own head, she saw a golden ladder appear immediately beneath the platform on which the rats had been standing.

Grenadine and Ruby could not believe their luck. They waded through the clay as quickly as they were able. It was not long before they reached the ladder, and they began hauling themselves up rung by rung. The weight of the clay on their clothes slowed them down a little, but they were determined to get to the top. They knew they might not get another chance.

Just as they were at the top, Augustus returned. 'Of course, I could make things easier still if you were to tell me where the jewel is, Ruby?' Ruby panicked. She had forgotten about the jewel. She hoped it was still in her pocket, as she had changed dresses. She did not know how, but she trusted that whoever dressed her in the tunnel had made sure the jewel had been protected. She tried to keep a straight face, so Augustus was unaware of her thoughts. She did not want him to get a hint that there might be a jewel in her possession.

Augustus teetered on the edge of the ladder, now threatening to land a big hairy foot on her hand. 'Your name is Ruby. It must be a Ruby you have. We are not totally stupid, us rats. Well, some of us are, but those of us who are on the Rat Council, namely me, Triston and Gumbert, are on the Rat Council because our intellectual capability. It is far superior to that of any other rats in this kingdom.'

Ruby was quick to respond. She did not want to get on the wrong side of Augustus or be pushed back into the clay pit. 'I know you are clever, Augustus. I can see by the way you speak to me. I do not have a Ruby. You are correct; I should have, but White Witch rules say that unless you have completed your White Witch training, you cannot carry a precious jewel. It is far too risky.'

Ruby was relieved to have thought of this White Witch lie so quickly. Augustus was flattered that Ruby thought him intelligent. He was quite often picked on by his brothers because he ate too much or was not as bright as they were. He decided she was telling the truth and allowed her to climb onto the shelf beside him.

At the top of the ladder and through the crack they were surprised to find a village. There were box-like coloured houses with glassless windows. As Ruby walked by each one, she got a closer look at the houses. She could see they were constructed of old rubbish, tins, plastic, bottles and polystyrene all melted together. The smell was unpleasant, but she thought the whole village quite ingenious. The rats were quite the little planet savers considering they were on the dark side, as they put it. She walked through some cobbled streets. The cobblestones were also made of rubbish. She could see a larger building at the top of a hill, which seemed to be where they were headed.

Triston said, 'The building at the top of the hill is the Town Hall. That is where we will be holding our masquerade this evening. It is an annual event, and all the rats who fund the Rat Council will attend. It is our way of saying thank you for the funding.'

Ruby nodded and smiled sweetly. 'How can we help?' she asked.

'Patience, child, all will become clear. We first need to make you look presentable. I assume you would like to bathe and change your clothes?'

Before she could answer, Grenadine spoke. She had been quiet up until this point. 'So long as you provide us with something tasteful to wear.'

Ruby cringed. She thought this might upset Triston. She snarled at Grenadine, trying to convey to her using facial expressions that she should think before speaking. Grenadine got the message. 'Of course, we would not like to appear ungrateful.' Ruby nodded encouragingly this time.

Triston looked Grenadine up and down. 'It looks to me that anything we offer would be an improvement on what you were wearing, even without the clay.' Ruby stifled a laugh.

There were rats busying about in all the streets they passed. Some on bicycles with shopping baskets full of litter. They were nearly knocked down by cycles on a couple of occasions.

Gumbert kept saying, 'Look out. Out of the way, stupid builders.' Perhaps they were in the middle of a building project—they were moving awfully fast. There were market stalls full of rotten fruit and vegetables, and some rats were selling 'lucky bags.' These were refuse bags seemingly full of rubbish but tied tightly so that the purchaser got a surprise when they opened it.

It was not long before they reached the door of the town hall. Augustus took a large golden key from his pocket and opened the door. They all walked inside. Grenadine and Ruby were at the back of the party, and at first they hesitated. Gumbert led them up a long spiral staircase. The staircase steps were polished white marble, and the bannister was heavy oak spindles. It was a wonderfully grand place if you could disregard that the main structure was made of recycled rubbish.

The first door they reached at the top of the stairs led them into a bedroom. There was a four-poster bed covered with a patchwork quilt in orange and blue.

'This is your room,' Gumbert said to Ruby. Ruby entered the room while Grenadine and Gumbert continued to the next room. Ruby thought the room looked welcoming and homey, not at all what she had expected. She tried to walk carefully across the floor. It looked expensive and was solid oak in keeping with the bed frame. Specks of clay and dust continued to fall onto the floor around her, a reminder of where she may end up if she did not do as the Rat Council asked. She opened the sturdy wardrobe's dense, heavy wood doors. There were pictures of rats on the doors. The wardrobe was empty except for one dress and a single pair of shoes. The dress was not the prettiest dress she had seen. It was almost ragged in its appearance and was dingy brown and grey colours with an asymmetrical hem, but it was clean and dry, so she was grateful. She walked into the bathroom adjacent to the bedroom. It too had white marble floors and walls and gold-coloured taps. The free-standing bathtub in the centre of the room had already been filled. Ruby undressed and placed her dirty clothes in a basket which sat next to the bath, but before she did, she checked for her ruby in the dress pocket. It was still there and still in its pouch. She filled the sink with soap and water and placed the ruby—still in the pouch—in the bowl to allow it to soak while she bathed. She locked the bathroom door, then stepped into the soothing water. Ten minutes passed, and she heard a rapping on the bedroom door. She stepped out of the bath quickly and began to get dressed. The dress was a little tight. Looking in the mirror she tried to straighten the creases. She squeezed the excess water out of the pouch, swilled the sink and pushed the pouch back in the pocket of her fresh dress. She straightened her hair with her fingers and slid into the shoes before she answered the door.

Triston stood in the doorway. 'Come to the kitchen and help prepare the food.' Ruby followed Triston back down the staircase. He continued to give instructions around the order of the evening and what would be expected from them. 'You will help prepare the food, serve the food and alcohol and meet any requests from the guests. Their happiness is crucial to the success of the evening and will ensure we remain on the Rat Council. Do not mess up. Do not be rude. Do not ask questions or answer back. You are our prisoners and our servants.'

Ruby nodded. 'Message received, loud and clear, sir.' She thought Triston's tone and delivery warranted a military-style response, as the instructions had seemed like orders.

'Okay, off you go,' Triston said.

Ruby entered the kitchen. There were people-sized rats everywhere, all preparing food on a large slate table. They seemed flustered and constantly bumped into each other as they tried to do one task or another. They were preparing vegetables, baking bread or cakes, whipping cream, stirring pans and filling glasses from a steaming brew in a cauldron. Ruby noticed Grenadine helping with the cheese. Chopping the cheese into all shapes and sizes. Ruby joined in with the preparations she began to chop fruit. After a few minutes, she saw Grenadine pass by, and she pulled on her sleeve. Grenadine leaned forward to hear Ruby.

'If you want out of here you will use your poison. You must not kill the rats, only send them to sleep. I will not be responsible for hurting the rats, whether I like them or not.'

Grenadine nodded. 'If you say so, but that takes a little of the fun out of it for me.'

Ruby looked over at the cauldron. Grenadine followed her gaze. 'Place your poison in the cauldron. We will keep refilling glasses until we are sure they have drunk enough to all go to sleep. We will then make our escape.'

Grenadine nodded and walked on. She did not want to bring attention to the fact that they were talking.

The guests seemed to enjoy the two visitors serving their food and drink, and as the night wore on, they got louder and drunker and more raucous in their behaviours. As planned, Ruby and Grenadine kept the cauldron punch flowing. Strangely, they made a great team. A scruffy set of the rats had gathered around Ruby to inspect her, raising the hem of her skirt and smelling her hair. She felt uncomfortable. The more irritated she looked and the more she pouted and pushed their paws away, the more they continued. She tried to curb her temper as she did not want to cause a scene. They were almost nearing completion of their plan. Some of the rats had already fallen asleep in their tall high-backed chairs. Some who had been playing chess in the corner of the room had fallen asleep with their heads resting on the table. There were at least ten rats still awake, including the Rat Council.

Augustus stood in the centre of the room. 'I would like to propose a toast to our guests. They have contributed to such a wonderful evening and have been such interesting serving staff. However, I think they have more to offer us in the form of entertainment. I propose Ruby join the remainder of the party and tell us all about life outside Validor. What a fascinating subject that would be! Who would like to hear stories of life on earth?'

The remaining rats mumbled something which sounded like they agreed, but the cauldron punch had begun to take effect, and none of them could speak coherently. Ruby told a long, dull story. She spoke slowly and dragged out the pronunciation of each word. She painted images of landscapes and grass and flowers where you could walk for miles in the sun, but nothing much happened. The less the rats knew of her world, the better.

There were four rats awake now. Slouched in their chairs but not quite asleep. She continued her story for as long as she could. Grenadine did not contribute. Now bored and weary she sat on the floor with her back pressed against the wall and her shoes kicked off.

Ruby shouted, 'Go!'

Grenadine almost jumped out of her skin. Ruby began rushing around the room grabbing the rats' tails and tying them together so that if the rats waked, they would not be able to chase her or Grenadine until they got themselves unknotted. Grenadine liked this game and started to help.

Once all the tails had been firmly tied together, they made their escape. Ruby looked across the room. She could see floor to ceiling stained glass windows with paintings of famous historic rats in them (or at least that is who Ruby assumed they were). The windows which were dressed in curtains of swags and tails. Swags and tails are a design of curtain which means they have a sweeping canopy at the top of the window with windows dropping down at either side, or at least that is how her mother explained them. However, in the Town Hall, swags and tails meant swags and tails—literally. There were several bags of 'swag' draped around the top of the window frame. The tails were actual cats' tails, which seemed to be moving even though not attached to a living animal.

The tails gave Ruby an idea. She would climb the tails up to the atrium, then break the glass and try to hop roof to roof to make her escape. Ruby had already worked out the position of each guard at every door who were easily recognisable by their heavy armour and swords. She ran over to the window, skidding on the marble floors. Grenadine followed, cackling with pride at their plan.

She scaled the opposite side of the window using the cat tails. Just as they smashed the atrium glass, Grenadine shouted,

'Thank you very much! We are not here all week.' She said it as though she had just come to the end of a stage show. She yelled, 'Yippee!' as they both swung out of the broken atrium windows. They realised neither of them really knew where they were going. All they could do is run. They jumped from roof to roof until their legs felt like they would collapse.

Just as they had both reached their breaking point, they leapt onto a roof which catapulted them into the air like the strongest trampoline in the world. They flew into the sky, so high they could no longer see the town below. They escalated higher and higher into the night sky. Their hair floating as though weightless. Then, they started to see white shapes getting closer. The shapes were clouds. 'My goodness, Grenadine. We have reached the clouds. We are actually in the clouds!'

# 20

# Dreams

When they arrived at the clouds, they could not hear a sound. The clouds were thick and dense and all the same white colour. Ruby placed a hand in front of her face. She could not see it. During their epic leap from Rat Pits, Ruby noticed they had joined hands, she was pleased. She realised Grenadine had made a few mistakes on their first meeting (Morganite had brought her up to speed), but Ruby had forgiven her. She decided one bad deed does not make a bad person.

Grenadine had helped Ruby so much in Rat Pits. This more than made up for the earlier mistakes. She wondered *when did they became friends, perhaps it was the Ruby working its magic?* Grenadine looked at their hands clasped together and smiled warmly at Ruby before letting go.

Ruby did not know what to do next. They were surrounded by thick clouds and fog and as far as she could tell, little else. Both tired now from the evening's events, so they curled up beside each other as if they were sheltering one another from whatever might come their way. The cloud wrapped itself around them matching each curve of their bodies and they gently drifted off to sleep.

Grenadine started to dream. She was now running through a forest and being chased by trees with no faces. Her heart raced as she tried to outmaneuver them, but they were quicker and striding confidently on a path they knew well. Grenadine slipped and stumbled and tripped on tree roots. Her feet were unsteady on the ground, and she feared it might not be long until one of the trees were able to catch her. Terror struck her. The trees were getting faster, as her feet felt heavier. She was surrounded. The branches wrapping around Grenadine's torso and legs. She started to scream out loud in her sleep.

Ruby awoke, startled to see Grenadine lying on the floor kicking and screaming. She did not know if she should wake her. Instead, she took the ruby out of her pocket and passed it across Grenadine's head. It seemed instinctive to her.

Grenadine settled and began to breathe more slowly. Her legs stopped kicking, and she was peaceful. Ruby tried to get back to sleep. Grenadine started to dream again. This time she could see large ancient trees. Her skin icy cold and covered in goosebumps. It got colder, so she began to rub her own naked skin to generate some warmth. She desperately looked around trying to find something she could use to cover herself. The trees still pushing her from one side to the other as if playing a game of forest pinball with a naked and scared Grenadine. Grenadine started to yell again, which woke Ruby once again. Each time Grenadine reached an extremely stressful situation in her dream, she began to shout in her sleep. Ruby knew exactly what to do this time and took her precious Ruby and passed it over Grenadine's head. Then she placed the Ruby back in her pouch and pocket. Grenadine seemed to relax again, so Ruby settled back into position and slept until morning came.

Ruby woke first and placed her hand on Grenadine's shoulder to awaken her. Grenadine opened her eyes, then sat up rather abruptly. 'What happened, where are we?'

'Your guess is as good as mine, Grenadine,' Ruby replied. Grenadine rubbed her eyes and looked around. "Did I talk in my sleep last night? I think I was having nightmares. I dreamed I was naked and being chased.'

Ruby smiled. She knew she had similar dreams, but found she now understood their meaning. It was as though the ruby had gifted her with the power to interpret dreams and (if needed) banish them. 'I can tell you what they mean if you would like,' Ruby said quietly, as she thought she might be ridiculed for such a bizarre ability.

'You can? I mean, I would really like to know,' said Grenadine enthusiastically.

'Very well,' Ruby answered. She told Grenadine that the dream of being chased probably means she is running from a buried truth. *Grenadine must suffer from fear and anxiety* Ruby thought. Ruby told Grenadine that she needs to acknowledge her feelings and make a change in her life so her mind can be at peace. The nakedness in the dream meant she was living a life different from the one she really wanted to live. Grenadine felt more relaxed now she understood herself a little more. She recognized some of the things Ruby was saying and thought it fascinating that Ruby had such a gift.

Grenadine thought about what she had heard. 'I think that could be true. I have never really liked being a Sable Witch. I am guilt-ridden when we cause things or people suffering or pain, but I was raised into the Sable Witch family, so it is who I am and who I must be.'

Ruby looked shocked. It was quite a revelation. She felt honoured that Grenadine had told her. 'Thank you for trusting me with your feelings, Grenadine. Please know that in this life you have choices. You can choose who you want to be and how you want to live your life, irrespective of what family you have been born into. If you are unhappy in life, you can choose a different path. I could help you with this.'

Grenadine liked the sound of a new and better life but did not think it possible. Sable Witches do not leave the Sable Witch Coven—at least not without consequences.

The fog had now disappeared, and they were surrounded by bumps in the clouds that looked like mini caves. 'Are they houses?' Grenadine asked.

Ruby shrugged her shoulders. There seemed to be hundreds of them. The whole place became a hive of activity. The area became cluttered with creatures that looked like walking balls of white fluff with stick-like legs and mouths. They had all started to move at once. Their colour exactly matching the clouds. They were also identical. They were rushing around from place to place, as though they had a purpose of which only they were aware.

Ruby began to strike up a conversation with one of them. They were moving so fast. She lined up with one of them and began to match its pace. 'Hi, I am Ruby, a new White Witch. I am visiting different places in Validor so that I can complete my White Witch training. Do you know where I should go next, or if there are any other White Witches here? In fact, can you tell me where I am?'

The white creature paused for a moment. 'Welcome White Witch Ruby. I am so pleased to meet you. We do not have any White Witches who actually live on Dream Cloud, but we have many who visit, usually to recover lost dreams.'

Ruby gave a grateful smile. 'Thank you for your help. Grenadine and I will ...' Before Ruby could finish her sentence, the white creature began to make a strange screeching noise. The noise attracted the other white creatures.

The first creature pointed at Grenadine and said, 'Beware! Beware, cloud creatures. We have a Sable

Witch in our vicinity! Panic ensued, and the funny little creatures started to rush around bumping into each other, without any purposeful direction. They were darting around giving Grenadine a wide berth.

Grenadine began to shake. She felt vulnerable and somewhat scared for her own safety. A hail of large frozen snowballs descended upon her; bypassing Ruby each time. Her legs stung when each one made contact. They felt like rocks. Solid and heavy, bouncing from one leg to the other before ricocheting to the floor. Grenadine tried to avoid them, but they started to land, thick and fast. She quickly looked around for shelter. There was nothing there. Ruby felt responsible as she had inadvertently alerted the cloud creatures to Grenadines presence. She felt a pang of guilt. Grenadine did not wish the creatures any harm and would probably love to be their friend.

Ruby decided she must do something. She started to climb to the top of one of the hills which she had thought were the cloud creatures' houses. She wanted to try to calm them but could only do this by climbing to the highest point and shouting to get their attention. Before she reached the top, a different female voice spoke over the chaos all around.

'Stop this. You know that not all Sable Witches have black hearts. Some are just born into the wrong families that have the wrong expectations about how they should live their lives. This is Dream Cloud. People who visit here can live out their dreams. They can start a different life just like I did. Let Grenadine tell us of the life she would like and then we can decide what to do.'

Ruby stretched on to her tip toes to get a closer look at the person talking. She saw a tall female with long red hair and a white fur cape. She wore a black long velvet dress. *It is a witch*, she thought but, *is she White or Sable?*. It is usually easy to tell if a witch is good or wicked because White Witches wear white and Sable Witches wear black. Every Witch with a different hair colour and or skin colour, but their clothes are always the giveaway. Witches wear the uniform of their Coven. So, judging by the clothes she wore, she was both.

Grenadine picked herself up from the ball she had made herself into on the floor. 'Greya? Is that you?' She rubbed her eyes.

'Yes, it is I, Grenadine. I live on Dream Cloud now. It was the only way I could be who I really felt I was. A good person and more of a White Witch than a Sable. The Coven would not accept me back, but I have a different family and friends now, and I am much more content.'

Grenadine rushed over and flung her arms around the woman's neck. 'Greya, I have missed you. I did not know where you went, and the Sable Coven would not tell me.'

Ruby had a confused look in her eye. She searched the ladies face for something which would help her identify who she was. The cloud creatures had stopped throwing the ice balls. They were watching and listening to the conversation between Grenadine and Greya. 'What happened and how did you get here'? 'It is such a long story and one I know I must owe you my dear sister, but first I must put an end to your pain and suffering whilst you are here.'

Grenadine stepped forward to speak to them, turning from side to side while she spoke so that her voice could be heard by all.

'I am sorry my family has struck fear in your hearts and this makes you want to hurt me without really knowing me. I am not here to harm you. I am like my sister—a good heart trapped in the wrong Coven. If you are angry at my people and need to direct your anger at me, then so be it. If it makes you feel better and corrects the Sable Witches' wrongs even for a moment, I will stand and allow you to continue. But I would much rather live with you and my sister harmoniously and help you protect your place in this world.'

Greya choked back the tears as the emotion of her sisters' heartfelt speech reached her. She could feel the sincerity pouring out of each word. The cloud creatures also seemed convinced of Grenadine's genuineness and began to drop the ice balls they had in their hands onto the floor. When their hands were free, some of them started to clap and others embraced. Greya's candid and brave words had moved them all.

• • •

The creatures returned to their homes and opened the white wooden doors that looked like they were attached to the frame of a furry igloo. They left the doors open as if to indicate they had accepted the Sable Witches into their hearts. Ruby, Grenadine and Greya thanked the cloud creatures for their hospitality and proposed that in the evening they should all meet again in the same place and talk some more.

The cloud creatures set off once again to complete their work. Ruby, Grenadine, and Greya lay their cloaks onto the floor and lit a fire—at least Grenadine did. Sable Witches were masters of fire and destruction, but this fire was to keep them all warm. She made the fire by rubbing her hands together and blowing into them. A white flame fired through the gaps in her fingers and onto the floor. Grenadine and Greya began to talk incessantly. It had been a long time, and they had so much to talk about. The shadow of dusk creeping in all around them, as the white creatures slowly reappeared and joined them by the roaring fire. The fire had grown now. It crackled quietly as if trying to encourage the creatures to come closer. A very welcoming sight for the cloud creatures after such a long day at work. Ruby puzzled on what these creatures did, but, decided today was not the time to ask.

One of the creatures sat next to Grenadine. 'When did you first realize that a Sable Witch life was not for you?'

Grenadine began to tell the story of her dreams and how Ruby had shown her that she could change. She talked of the dream being a message from a higher authority that all was not well in her life and that it was time to be the person she wanted. The dream creatures enjoyed the story, as they were living in a place where forgotten dreams were relived, and they were the proud gatekeepers for this; it fit into their whole purpose in life. They were keen to learn more about Ruby's dream interpretation powers. Some of them offered reoccurring dreams they had been experiencing in the hope that Ruby might be able to translate them.

One of the creatures started to talk of reoccurring dreams of flying an aeroplane and losing control of the plane. Several other creatures were amazed, as they had had the same dream.

'That type is a familiar dream to many people. It means that something is holding you back and stopping you from moving forward in life. It can also mean that you are struggling with keeping up with the goals you have set for yourself, or perhaps you lack confidence. You should have confidence that you can do what you set out to do and push away self-doubting thoughts. Remember, they are just thoughts. You can achieve anything you want.'

The cloud creatures were excited at Ruby's insight, and they were chattering away with each other in separate conversations about their dreams and what they might mean. Another said to Ruby, 'Sometimes, I dream I am falling. What would you make of that?'

Ruby knew that was also a dream about anxiety and insecurity. She explained that perhaps there was a change happening in their life that was out of their control. 'If you are content to be falling in the dream, it means you do not fear the change and are going with the flow. Dreams often reflect what we need, who we really are, and what we value in life.'

Another female voice from behind Ruby whispered, 'What if you are sad because long ago, someone took your powers, so you dream of a time when you have your powers? When you awaken, you realise the only way you could possibly regain your lost powers is to come to the Dream Cloud because just for a short time you can be anyone you want to be?'

Ruby recognized the voice immediately. She turned around to see her mother. She yelped with happiness, and they hugged and kissed. 'But how?'

Amber replied, 'This is where I go on vacation. It is the only way I get to experience the full magic that I would have inherited if Grandma Sylvia had not made her mistake. It is such a fun time for me and today it is also a great way to check up on you. You look well. You have made some new friends, I see,' she said, as she cast her eyes across the cloud creatures.

Ruby nodded, excited to see her mother again. Amber tried to manage her expectations. 'It is so lovely to see you, but you must know that you still have many places to visit before your training is complete. I cannot be there for those visits but be assured I have many people keeping a watchful eye over you to ensure you do not come to any harm.'

Ruby knew that was true. 'Grenadine has a White Witch heart under the Sable Witch exterior, and we have had many adventures together'.

Grenadine heard the conversation and decided she should join in. 'Ruby, you have changed my life. I have my sister back, and I can now live without the horrid influence of the remaining Sable Witch family. However, it does mean I must stay here on Dream Cloud. There will be terrible consequences if I return to the Sable Witch realms and Coven. I hope you can understand?'

A melancholic expression passed over Ruby's face. 'I understand, but I do not look forward to roving alone.'

Amber rested a reassuring hand on Ruby's shoulder. 'I will help you find your way to the next realm. Now, get some sleep, as tomorrow you will leave for the next part of your journey.'

After a delicious breakfast of pancakes and syrup that Amber prepared for her the next morning, Ruby was keen to know where she must visit next and how she might get there.

Amber pointed to the clouds floating above her head. 'If you look at each cloud closely, you will see that they form shapes. Most people do not notice, but for at least half a second, those shapes tell you what the future will be.'

Ruby reeled in astonishment. She thought clouds were just something formed because of the weather.

Amber pointed to the clouds above their heads. 'Tell me what you see. Focus your mind.' Ruby looked up at the clouds moving at what seemed to be a snail's pace above their heads. At first, she saw nothing, but randomly shaped clouds and impatience crept in but, then she saw them. Bat shapes and caves. She thought she must be imagining it.

'I know this must sound strange, but I see bats and caves.'

Amber looked nervous. 'Okay, you are going to a place named Blankinsa Caves. It is a most dangerous place, as it is pure Sable Witch territory. I do not want to frighten you; I only want you prepared as you must be strong. You will be tested to your limits. You have everything you need to navigate through safely to the next place. Do not lose confidence and trust your instincts. Do only good things, and you will not go wrong.'

Ruby did not like the sound of Blankinsa Caves and did not want to let her mother down. 'So, this is goodbye again?'

'For now,' Amber replied, holding her tightly. 'Just for a short while.'

Ruby felt ready but did not know how to start. Amber pointed upwards.

'Follow the clouds you saw. They will take you directly there.'

Amber straightened her daughter's cloak and turned her to face the sea of clouds.

'Go get them,' she said in a light-hearted way.

Even though she knew the Blankinsa Caves were so dark and dismal that everyone who visited went into a dark depression and some never returned. She felt Ruby was different somewhat, stronger maybe-or more courageous?. She watched Ruby head off into the distance. Telling herself, *she will get through this and return home soon.*

Ruby looked up to the sky. There was the bat-shaped cloud. She began to follow it.

# 21

# Blankinsa Caves

Ruby stayed focused on the cloud above her. Carefully and deliberately placing each foot making sure to stay on track. She did this for what seemed like an eternity across the fog-like texture of Dream Cloud. It felt springy and soft beneath her feet. Then, without warning she stepped on something and in so doing, she flicked it into the air. She could not see what it was, but it landed a hundred yards or so away from where she stood. She made her way over to the mysterious object on the ground.

As she got closer, Ruby realised it looked like a tiny little person with wings. She could not see if it was a boy or a girl. It had a silver bodysuit which may have been its skin. Even the head and what might have been hair covered by the silver skin. The creature had a silver face and big gold oval eyes. The eyes were kind and cat-like. The creature did not appear to have a mouth. The wings were delicate and transparent and had vein-like lines running through them which were also silver in colour. Ruby picked up the tiny winged creature; It fit comfortably in the palm of her hand.

'What are you? The creature sat up in the palm of her hand. Ruby did not get a reply, but she realised she already knew the answer. It's a fairy! She did not understand how she knew it was a fairy or why it was here. The answer came to her in an instant.

'You are here to guide me to Blankinsa Caves.'

The creature stood on its feet, then flew into the hood of her cape and lifted Ruby into the air. Ruby could no longer see the fairy, but she knew it was the reason she began rising rapidly from the ground, higher by the second. *How did it know which direction to go?* Again, Ruby seemed to know the answer as soon as she thought the question. The fairy had a special gift to be able to navigate to any place. The pulses created in its suit made this happen. It was like sonar for a bat or submarine.

Ruby began to understand. The fairy sent the words into Ruby's head. She found this unsettling. It made her question everything. When was a thought truly hers, if ever? Her head hurt. She decided to park the analysis for a while and concentrate on her journey. The views were spectacular. Mountains, fields, lakes, corn, sunflowers and crops a beautiful large-scale landscape painting lying right beneath her. They flew together for miles and miles. She was so high; she could not see anyone beneath her. It was bright and dry at first, so she had a clear view of the breathtaking scenery, and then the sky turned grey, and the air began to feel cool on her skin.

Below her, the scenery had changed. The ground looked like black ash, some of which still seemed to be burning. She could see smoke and glowing embers in some places. She imagined if you tried to walk across it, it would burn your feet. It also seemed to be moving in some places.

They started to drop lower and lower. Ruby didn't like the look of the fairy's chosen landing spot, but there was nothing she could do. As they dropped, she could see caves carved into the walls of a volcano. Perhaps this was the reason for the ash and embers. It was lava which had once erupted from the volcano. Maybe that was why the ground appeared to be moving?

As they got closer to the ground, she realised the lava appeared to be moving but, it was not lava. It was masses of spiders scuttling on the ground close to the volcano. She shuddered. She did not like spiders! This place looked like her worst nightmare. Her feet now touching the ground. The fairy deposited her at the opening to one of the caves. Ruby knew the fairy would leave her now, as Blankinsa caves was no place for fairies.

Ruby thanked the fairy and watched the unusual creature fly away faster than the speed of light. She felt alone. Trying to refocus she looked for a way into the cave. She tentatively stepped into the dark and stale smelling cave entrance. There were icicles hanging high up in the cave walls, and she could see particles of water dripping from the icicles occasionally. The drips made a popping sound as they hit the puddles which had formed beneath them. Ruby tried to avoid the puddles as her footwear was made of lace and not waterproof. She could hear nothing except for the sound of dripping water.

She decided to try the magic trick she had witnessed in Hope Coast. She clapped her hands together, blew into them and instantly she had a tiny ball of fire in her palm. Pleased she had paid attention to Morganite when he performed this magic. It seemed there were some pieces of magic that were common to all White Witches, and this was one of them.

Ruby could see a little better but not the entire cave. The light from the fire showed her where to place her feet. As she walked further into the grey and craggy cave, she could hear animal sounds. She thought it might be birds. She reached an area at the end of a long narrow cave corridor which looked like a little room. A large crowd of bats circled around her head and body in an uncoordinated fashion. They were chattering to each other, talking over each other. She could not decipher one conversation from another.

'Get out of the way you nincompoop' one said.

'You are in my way, stupid,' said another.

'Does anyone know where they are going in this place?'

'Look out, look out! Coming in!'

'Left, left! I said, left!'

The noise now deafening and Ruby really did not want to get hurt. The bats were flying awfully close, and they would often brush her cheek or hair with

147

their wings. She completely lost her orientation. She found herself writhing and jerking to try and avoid them. She flicked them out of her hair. When she found the opportunity, she looked around. She saw a whole room filled from top to bottom with bats. There were stepped ledges in the cave walls that looked like walking gantries, but the walkways were not in use. She slammed her hand on the cave wall in frustration. *How long must I endure this circus* she thought.

Ruby heard a 'Psst!' She could not see where the sound had come from. She heard the sound again. This time she looked to the first gantry close to her. She felt completely horrified by what she saw.

It was a spider, a large, red spider with bright blue eyes. All eight of them.!

'Hurry, hurry. I is Spinaka, I helps you.' Her bottom lip began to quiver in fear.

It spoke in a strange version of English. Ruby tried to think of ways to politely decline. This was an eerie and dangerous-looking spider and almost the same size as her. He had long skinny legs and nobly knees, six on each leg. His body covered in fur, and each tiny hair sticking straight up. Ruby eyed him cautiously. 'How do I know you won't hurt me?'

The spider looked uneasy. His eyes looked shifty now and an insincere half-smile crossed his face. 'Spinaka helps Ruby. Come, come. Follows me. I knows the way. Who else can helps you?' the spider said with a sneaky smile. Ruby remained unconvinced by his attempted charm. There was something about this spider she did not like, but she knew she had no other option, and the spider knew it too.

She pulled herself onto the first ledge next to the spider. 'Okay, lead the way Spinaka' she said resigned to the fact that she must follow this odd spider. Spinaka started to scurry along the lowest gantry. He stopped for a moment and lifted his bottom to face upwards. He released a thick line of web which immediately hit its target, the next gantry.

'Climbs now,' he said.

Ruby gripped the line of web and shimmied up as best she could. It stuck to her fingers, but that helped keep her hands and feet on the line. She reached the second gantry. Once Spinaka was sure she reached the next level, he removed the web and started again. They repeated the climb three times until they reached the fourth gantry. Eventually reaching a cave doorway.

Spinaka looked sneaky again, and his eyelids looked heavy. 'Afters you,' he said, bowing to allow Ruby to pass through the door.

She walked into another cave room. The floor moved in front of her, it was a carpet of small rainbow coloured spiders this time. They were crawling across her feet. She froze on the spot with fear and began to feel sick. They did not attempt to climb higher than feet level, so she relaxed her now tense muscles a little. She could see a stone staircase on the other side of the room which led to what looked like a wide platform. She swallowed and began to shuffle through them, as she did not want to hurt them or be hurt by them. This took some time and careful footwork, but she eventually got to the foot of the stairs.

Spinaka had not followed her. He stood in the doorway where they had entered the cave. Ruby stood still at the foot of the stairs when she heard a crack of what sounded like thunder. The room filled with smoke and the spiders scattered to the sides of the room. A path appeared and began to divide them. Once the smoke cleared, Ruby could see someone at the top of the stairs. She could make out a red dress and red high-collared cloak and long fair hair. It was a man. He had a tall red and gold crown on his head, and a red net veil trailed from the crown. The spiders were knelt on the floor face down and motionless. She knew this must be someone important.

'Ruby of Braeriach,' the man said. 'I am King Organza; I am the King of the Sable Witch Coven.' He started to glide gracefully down the stairs towards her. 'You are a silly girl; why would you trust a spider? You are now my prisoner.'

Ruby panicked. She needed to find her way out of here! She must reach the doorway on the other side of the room. She now understood why the spider did not move away from the doorway. King Organza stepped closer. She darted from side to side and Organza mirrored her movements.

'Leave me alone-I do not want to fight!' She shouted.

'How pathetically weak, so like a White Witch, all show and no go!' he sneered.

'Don't you understand? You will become invaluable to me if I keep you here and make my demands to the White Witch Coven.' He stroked his long blond hair while speaking. 'I will tell them that the only way to ensure your release is if they all come to Blankinsa Caves to retrieve you in person. I will have the whole

White Witch Coven, and I will trap them here and make sure they can never return to their homes and lives. I will hold all the power, and every part of Validor will become a Sable Witch realm.'

Ruby knew she must do everything she could to make sure that did not happen. When Organza finally reached her, Ruby pulled her jewel from her pocket. She began to wrestle with Organza, trying to get him to the ground. Organza was at least six feet six in height, and Ruby was only five feet six inches. Organza pinned Ruby to the floor and appeared to be working magic with his eyes. A ray of light radiating from them onto Ruby's face. She squeezed her eyes together and managed to overpower Organza for a moment. She held his hair with one hand and pressed the ruby to his forehead with the other and as she did, Organza stopped fighting. He looked dazed.

'What am I doing here? Ruby, my friend, are you okay?'

The ruby had worked! Organza behaved like a long-lost friend. *How long will the power of the ruby last* she thought. She knew if she kept it close to him the magic would not wear off. So, she must capitalize on this. 'HI, Organza. Thank you for the invite to your cave. What a lovely place it is. I have enjoyed my time here, but I need to move to the next town. Perhaps you could help?'

The spiders were confused, but Ruby felt sure they would do whatever Organza wanted. Organza is a wicked King and had fried many of their spider families in the past when they had not given him what he demanded.

'Of course, Ruby. Spinaka will show you out. He makes a great guide and knows my caves so well. Have a safe journey.' With that, Organza turned and walked back obliviously up the staircase. Ruby did not need to be asked twice. Afraid the magic might wear off. She made her way back to the doorway. Spinaka met her there and began to walk her through the corridors of the caves as quickly as he could. He did not want to disobey Organza.

They travelled gantry after gantry, corridor after passage. It seemed like a long way, and Ruby started to think they might be lost. An identical spider arrived.

'Hi, Spinaka, what are you doing in the north passages? I do not often see you here.' This spider had a warmer face, and it looked less mischievous in nature.

'Hi, Solomon. I thinks I is in South passages. I may have lost my ways. Spinaka lay down on the floor and placed two of his spindly spider legs over his eyes. 'Oh no, Organza is be mads at me. I need to lead Ruby outs of the caves.'

Solomon patted Spinaka on the head.

'Easy mistake to make, my friend. Let me help. Follow me, Ruby. Spinaka you must find your way back. You must be tired.'

Spinaka began to hurry away before he changed his mind. He looked back and yelled.

'Thank you, Solomon,' he replied and scuttled off into the corridor.

Solomon started to walk in front of Ruby, and she knew she should follow. 'This way,' he said in a no-nonsense kind of way. Ruby knew she could trust him. He had a kind face and seemed more together than Spinaka. They soon reached the cave mouth and familiar surroundings—the bed of ash and embers. Solomon realised Ruby would not be able to cross the hot ash, so he lay on the floor.

'Climb on my back,' he said. She lifted her skirt and threw her leg across his wide body. She sat upright and Solomon started to move. At first he moved slowly. Then quickly picked up the pace, his long legs gliding across the dust covered ash at high speed. The ash seemed to stretch for miles, but Ruby could see in the distance what looked like a long and winding stream which stretched from the opposite side of Blankinsa Caves. They were headed for the water. It seemed to stretch to the end of Validor and looked spectacular, even from a distance.

On first glance, they saw a fast running stream, but it was not filled with water. It was brimming with something resembling liquid gold. Solomon stopped and crouched down.

'This is where I must leave you. My home is in Blankinsa Caves. I am afraid I would not survive for too long in the sun.' Ruby understood. She was grateful for Solomon's help. He stood back up and was about to trot back in the direction of the cave when the current from the stream caused a giant wave to splash over the banks of the stream. It lifted Solomon from the edge and dropped him into the unstoppable current.

Ruby tried to grip his leg, but it slipped out of her hand. Solomon drifted down the stream, further and further away. Rolling one way and then the other. Ruby wondered how he would survive. Her heart sank. She blamed herself. If Solomon had not been trying to help her, he would not have been anywhere close to the stream. She began to cry for a moment but was distracted by the sight of a large bird-like animal flying in the sky headed towards the stream. It was green and scaly with red eyes. A dragon! Ruby thought they only existed in stories, but here it was, living, breathing and flying!

The dragon flew slowly and deliberately, its wings powerful and sure. It swiftly reached Solomon. Ruby watched in awe as the magnificent creature dived into the stream, grabbed Solomon's leg and lifted him into the sky. The dragon swooped around and headed back to join Ruby. When he reached her, he landed gracefully on the ground. A stunning animal, truly majestic and strong in build. He released an out of breath Solomon.

'How can I ever repay you?' Solomon said. The dragon lifted the corners of his mouth in a smile but did not speak. Solomon turned to Ruby. 'This is Nodrog, the keeper of the golden stream. He will help you on your journey. I must go now. I do not want to end up somewhere I should not be again. Good luck, Ruby!' This time Solomon sprinted much faster in the opposite direction and away from the stream banks.

Ruby began to stroke Nodrog. 'Thank you, Nodrog. You are my hero.' Nodrog rubbed his head against her body, almost knocking her sideways.

She smiled at him affectionately and patted him caringly on the head to say thank you. Nodrog lifted Ruby onto his shoulders, preparing her for flight. He launched into the air confidently but leisurely, navigating the airwaves and rising and falling as he did. Ruby could feel the wind brushing her face like a feather. As they moved further from the caves, the sun began to peep through the grey clouds until they were entirely gone. This time Ruby could see acres of forest. They reached a clearing, and as they travelled across it, she saw many tiny mud huts. They were all shapes and sizes, and some were on stilts. They were brown and green as they were made from a mixture of mud and reeds. They looked like they had all been hand made without any design or measurements.

Nodrog started to drop down towards the village. She could see a large archway which had a sign carved into the wooden arch. It said Trust Town.

# 22

# Trust Town

Nodrog used his expert navigation skills to fly them through the arch. Now close to ground level but not quite there. He glided through the streets of the unassuming village. Ruby noticed the village had a mud floor and lush greenery all around. It looked to be a simple place. They reached a building larger than the others; it looked as though four huts had been glued together with a walkway between each one.

Nodrog touched the ground next to the door of the hut. The door slightly ajar. A face peered from around it as if to check if it was safe to venture out. A short man appeared. He had caring but tired features and laughing eyes. He had a mass of untidy, shoulder-length white hair and wore a long, shiny purple and yellow patchwork coat with large brown stitching on each patch. He carried a walking stick. He had large leather boots on, which looked a tad too big for him and the laces were undone and trailing on the floor as he hobbled. An old pair of spectacles perched precariously on his head.

'Good work, Nodrog. I have some of your favourite gumballs in the hut. Go and help yourself,' he said to the dragon. Nodrog poked his head inside. The man walked over to Ruby now and began to inspect her through his tiny glasses. He pulled a magnifying glass out of his coat to get a closer look. This made Ruby feel on edge, but he seemed harmless.

'Hmm, you look like Amber, and you fit the description. You must be Ruby. I am Professor Clapton. Please come into my humble abode.'

Ruby felt relieved he had put away the magnifying glass. 'Hello, Professor. It is nice to meet you,' she replied.

The Professor had already turned to hobble back into his house. He had not waited for or expected a reply from Ruby.

She followed him inside and noticed plants growing up the fingerprint clad walls. They were in large wooden plant boxes sitting close to the walls. In the first room they came to there were four large steel boxes which were taller than they were. They looked to be propping each other up and resembled gambling machines. The type you might find in an amusement arcade. They passed through the room and reached another which had beautiful windows letting in copious amounts of natural light. They were sash windows.

Some of them were open, and rubber hoses were draped outside.

The hoses were attached to a series of bubbling chemicals held in the largest beakers and test tubes she had ever seen holding green and red liquid. Some filled with transparent water-like liquid. Ruby and Professor Clapton passed through the second room. Then another followed. The third room looked rather like a hall of mirrors you might see at an amusement park or in a circus. Ruby quickly moved on. This room was empty. There were several doors around the room, which perhaps led to somewhere. Professor Clapton went to a large green door and opened it. He and Ruby walked through the door, and Ruby found herself in an all-white room—a white bed, white carpet, white curtains, white walls, white draws, white hearts floating from the ceiling on white strings and white candelabras.

'This is the white guest room. It is your room as long as you stay with me,' Professor Clapton said in a high-pitched voice. Ruby loved the cleanliness of the room. She followed the professor back. Ruby found herself in a rather untidy kitchen. In the corner, she noticed Nondog's head coming through the window. His chin rested on a large bean bag while he crunched his way through his beloved gumballs.

There were contraptions everywhere in the kitchen. Each looked to be used to prepare or cook food. A large grey stove sat at the back of the room with a simmering pot on it. Ruby could not see every item in the room. It was extremely cluttered. There were pipes, springs, weights, clocks, scoops, spoons, tins, bowls, pans, pots, spices, chopping boards, metal containers, hooks and knives all littered in various places in a cluttered and unorganized way. Ruby couldn't imagine how Professor Clapton knew where everything was. He pulled out a steel stool next to a matching table in the centre of the room.

'Please sit down. I have some supper prepared; you must be hungry.'

It had been some time since she had eaten. She had not been too hungry, and there had been many distractions. Still unaware of the beetles' magical juice that had been administered while she slept back at Lightning Pass. The food smelled delicious, the aroma of pot content filled her nostrils and made her eager to taste it.

Professor Clapton took some bowls from the floor and placed them onto the table near the stove. He grabbed a wooden chopping board and selected a large knife from the rack hanging in front of him. He went to the oven and opened its doors. At first, a large billow of smoke blasted into his face. He reached into the oven and pulled out a large loaf of bread. He took the bread to the table and began slicing it into pieces on the chopping board. He returned to the stove and using a ladle started to scoop pea and ham soup into each bowl. She had made it before with her mother. It was a favourite of hers.

Ruby broke the silence. 'I love pea and ham soup. It is my mother's favourite too.' The professor stopped scooping the soup for a moment and looked into the distance as if remembering something painful.

'Yes, I know. I know your mother, Ruby. We, well, we, we were once friends, a long time ago.'

Ruby smiled. Comforted by the fact that the professor knew her mother. It was nice to meet someone who understood who she was and where she came from. She spooned the soup into her mouth as quickly as she could and dipped the large chunks of fresh bread into it. This soup tasted better than her mother's, despite the professor's chaotic approach to making it.

'This is the best soup I ever tasted,' Ruby said enthusiastically.

Professor Clapton laughed. 'Best not to tell your mother. I am also a scientist and a chemist. You need to understand chemistry to be a good cook!'

'How do you know my mother, Professor?' Ruby asked.

She had finally plucked up the courage to ask. Even if at an inappropriate moment.

The professor looked at the floor. A gloomy expression inhabiting his face. 'I met your mother many years ago. Long before you were born. I met her in Little Love Forest one summer evening...' He began to tell Ruby the story of how he met Amber. He was a woodcutter in Little Love Forest. She was nearing the completion of her White Witch training. They spent one long hot summer together and became great friends. They had so much in common. They liked nature and science and would often study the stars together. They were both trying to learn about astronomy and other galaxies. It was on one of the nights that they were studying the stars through a large telescope that they first kissed. They fell in love. Ruby heard how inseparable they had become, spending every waking moment together, until disaster struck.

A Sable Witch saw them in the forest and cast a spell which meant the next bout of rain would fall on the professor, and he would become different. 'You should know that when Sable Witches create rain using evil magic, it is referred to as 'black rain.' The magic within the black rain would be different according to the skills of the witches who created it. It inevitably results in the victim becoming confused and delusional.'

In the professor's case, he became controlling, and he would not let Amber out of his sight. He did not trust her even to speak to other people. Amber felt heartbroken inside. She did not know how to bring the man she first met back to her. She had no choice but to flee Little Love Forest. One of the saddest parts of the story is that although the professor had turned into a different person to the one she had met, he did love her so very much and had never intended to hurt her. She gave him so much joy he would not let her leave.

Ruby wondered why her mother had never mentioned Professor Clapton and started to worry if he would try to hold her there too? The professor continued with his story. He had since spent his life building Trust Town piece by piece with his own hands. It was a place where anyone who had been rained on by black rain could be treated. He had researched the rain and its impact on people for many years and eventually found the antidote. That was the reason for all the machines and test tubes. His life's work and years of research born out of a broken heart.

'Did you ever meet my mother again and tell her what you had found?'

The professor shook his head. 'I did not want to cause your mother any more pain. My mission in life is to make sure that no one else would ever lose the one great love of their life because of the black rain.'

The professor jumped out of his chair. 'Now, enough of the chit chat. We must help you along with your mission. Come with me.'

Ruby followed him out of the room of chemicals and into the room of mirrors. She faced each mirror, and sure enough, they each made her look strange. First, she looked fat, then thin, then long, then short, then her face looked upside down and all her features were in the wrong place like in a Picasso picture. Then in the last mirror, the professor asked her to look closely. Ruby leaned forward, and in the blink of an eye, eight arms reached out of the mirror. She jumped back, but they managed to reach her. The arms were long and spaghetti-like. They started to tickle her. She laughed so much; her belly hurt.

'Please stop, my tummy hurts.' The professor stepped in. 'Cease, mirrors.' The arms retracted back into the mirror.

Ruby managed to regain her composure. 'What is this room? Another scientific experiment?'

'No, indeed not. This is just for fun. It helps me not take life too seriously. This is where I come to unwind; it is my playroom. My scientific studies are such a chore sometimes, and this is my way to relax!'

Ruby liked this idea. It was the professor's escape. She was pleased he had found a way to smile whilst he was completing such important work. They laughed together and left the room. The professor led her into the room with the doors and began to explain the room's purpose.

'As you would expect, each door leads somewhere. Some are rooms in my house, as you have already discovered, while others are doors to different parts of Validor. Each White Witch has a learning programme set for them. They do not know what it is, but the White Witch Coven does. That means that when the time is right, and you are ready, you will select the door that is meant for you. The door to another part of Validor.'

Ruby pulled a face, disappointed that things had gotten so serious again, but she knew she must follow the path that had been set for her. 'What if I pick the door to another room in your house?'

'You will only pick the wrong door if you are not ready. It simply means you will wait another day because you're learning in Trust Town is not complete,' the professor explained. 'Are you ready?' he asked.

Ruby nodded. 'Well, I guess I am going to find out' she replied. The professor gestured towards the door. Ruby stepped in front of each door, hesitating at each one-trying to let her intuition tell her which to open. She did not feel any different irrespective of which one she touched. She decided to just pick one.

She opened the door slowly and stepped through it. She could see a frozen lake in the middle of an area filled with pebbles. The pebbles crunched under her feet when she changed her weight from one side of her body to the other. The ice looked black and dangerous.

The atmosphere was gloomy and grim. She could see the full circumference of the lake and bare grey trees that looked to be dying as if the frost had taken every bit of their life force. They were broken and in strange shapes probably from the strong icy wind. The cold bit into her skin and frost formed on her hands and cheeks. She had lost the feeling in her mouth, and her teeth began to chatter with the cold. She was sure her lips were frozen. She turned to look for the door. A part of her had hoped she had stepped through the wrong door. The doors had disappeared. There were strange-looking trees surrounding the lake. She had no inkling of where she might be, but she suspected she would need to be alert. This did not feel like White Witch territory.

# 23

# Ice Valley

Ruby noticed the elderly trees were moving, so slowly it was almost unnoticeable. Ruby strained her eyes to make sure she didn't imagine it. The trees were moving towards her. At first, they crossed the land on which they looked to have been rooted until it looked like they were standing on the black ice of the lake. It took a few moments before she truly understood what the tree shapes had become. The gnarled broken looking trees were not trees, they were Dark Shadows-they fit the exact description she once heard during a conversation with Grenadine, and all of them had stepped onto the lake. Ruby was surrounded. They came closer. Now petrified and frozen to the spot without the need of the cold to help it along. She knew if she had the courage, she could move. The sheer terror of the whole situation holding her back.

One of the Dark Shadows tossed a solid object across the ice towards her. She hoped it would not break the ice as she was afraid to find herself beneath it in sub-zero temperatures. The object stopped sliding and she could see a wooden hockey stick. Ruby looked around at the Dark Shadows around her. They had masks on that served to disguise and protect them. They were unlike any hockey mask she had seen before. They were more like solid wood masks which covered the Dark Shadows' faces; there were eye holes and air holes, but no other facial features were on display. The eyes were not familiar. Their eyes were animal-like, almost predatory, black from top to bottom with a bright red dot in the centre. The red dot lit up, bright and laser-like.

Ruby saw that they all had hockey sticks, but they were not moving. They were standing on the ice in a semi-circle surrounding Ruby, their hockey sticks placed firmly on the ice. They were waiting for something. A shrill whistling noise could be heard above them. Each one ducked. Ruby did not know what to do, but she followed their lead. She heard a crash on the ice. She saw a shiny flat black stone sitting close to where the crash noise had come from. It had not broken the ice on the landing but had created a hairline crack.

Ruby knew she needed to get to the other side of the lake as quickly as possible, but she guessed the Dark Shadows would not let her do that without a fight. Their chosen fight in this instance was an ice hockey match. Ruby had played field hockey but never ice hockey. She knew that ice hockey should also involve ice hockey boots but saw that the dark creatures did not have any. They had dirty duck-like feet with something resembling suction pads underneath, while Ruby had only her lace shoes.

The stone started to move on its own. The dark creatures were watching its path intently. They attempted to follow it, the suckers on their feet making a slurping sound each time they moved, latching and unlatching from the ice, causing them to move in a jerky manner.

Ruby lost interest in the game. She had a different objective in mind. She only wanted to reach the other side safely and unharmed. She started to slide her feet over the ice tenuously. First, the left foot, followed by the right. She was not headed for the hockey game. The Dark Shadows continued in their tournament, untroubled by Ruby's presence on the ice. They used quite a force to knock her out of the way in passing. Each one deliberately banging her with their shoulders or clipping her ankles with their hockey sticks. Ruby cried out in pain. She felt sure they could not see her.

Occasionally the force of their impact on her body knocked her to the ice. She would find herself on her bottom or on her hands and knees, winded and gasping for breath. Each time she got back to her feet, unwavering in her mission to reach the other side of the lake. She felt sore, battered, bruised and exhausted. The creatures hit the stone among themselves. There was a thwack each time the stone met the stick. An incredible force behind each stroke of the hockey stick. Ruby knew if the stone should hit her ankle in the wrong way at close range, it would likely shatter her bones. Just as the thought arrived in her head, she heard a crack.

The stone had hit her ankle. For a fleeting moment she felt nothing, then the pain engulfed her, making her sick to the stomach. The other side now in sight. She would not be defeated. She hopped on her good foot, sometimes slipping over onto the merciless ice and having to start again.

She reached the other side, and it was only then that the creatures appeared to notice her. The let out the strangest gargling sound from their throats. They raised their hockey sticks above their heads and began to run towards her, their suckers making a thwupping sound with each step they took. Ruby dragged herself to a flat piece of ground next to the ice. She looked around, thinking quickly. She could only see more trees, so she shuffled around to face them.

'Trees, if any of you are carrying my Grandma Sylvia's magic, I could really use some help right now!'

The stones crunched beneath the Dark Shadows hooves; Ruby could hear their menacing heavy breathing. Now struck with terror and convinced she could feel the warmth of their pungent breath on her face. The crunching grew louder-slowly reaching a crescendo. Then *Whoosh* in the blink of an eye the creatures are caught in the tree's branches. The trees now wrapping themselves around their gnarled, lumpy torsos in a ropelike lasso. Ruby exhaled the breath she had held for what seemed like a lifetime. She knew she did not have much time. The ugly creatures might find the strength to escape. She began to crawl as quickly as her knees and now strained wrists could carry her.

# 24

# Little Love Forest

R uby sat for a moment. She had limped far enough
to feel the dark shadows had lost track of her. There
were trees all around her, their leaves green and lush,
unlike the trees she had left behind at the lakeside. Her
ankle still swollen and sore from its brief encounter with
the hockey stone, but she breathed a sigh of gratitude at
reaching the other side of the lake and having the chance
to resume her journey. The weather was also different
here warmer, and she could see tiny flowers peeping their
delicate heads through the grass, stretching so they could
feel the warm sun on their golden faces. The grass long
and green, and when she had walked through it kissed
her ankle as if in sympathy. It felt like springtime—fresh
and crisp. She began to talk herself into getting up and

walking again; her ankle still throbbed, and she was wondered how far she must travel.

She heard a clatter of wooden wheels hitting the pebbled path she had crossed over on her way from the lake. Whatever it was, it was moving at quite a pace. She knew that, friend or foe, she would not be able to outrun it. Then she saw it—a beautiful golden carriage on wooden wheels. It was a royal carriage drawn by four large stallions with black glossy coats and manes. On top of the horses' heads were red feather headdresses. Their saddles were black and gold, and a gentleman sat on the edge of the carriage holding the horse's reigns. He wore a top hat and waistcoat. His hair was curly and grew down the sides of his face, covering his odd-shaped ears.

When he saw Ruby, he pulled the horses' reigns towards him, and they came to a halt.

'Good day, young lady. Would you like to take the carriage to Little Love Forest?' he asked in a matter-of-fact way. Ruby looked him up and down inspecting him for signs of wickedness. She decided to take a chance as her ankle seemed to be getting worse and now resembled a deflated balloon. She managed to push herself off the ground using her wrists without putting too much stress on her damaged leg, and she limped over to the carriage. The door opened in front of her. She leaned into the carriage and saw White Witch Morganite on one side of the carriage.

Ruby had never been so relieved to see someone in all her life. 'Morganite, you are a sight for sore eyes, or a sore ankle in my case.!'

Morganite responded with a hug. 'Oh, do get in, Ruby. I have been looking for you!' Ruby did not need to be asked a second time, and with a helping hand from Morganite clambered into the crushed red velvet seats of the carriage. Morganite leaned out of the window. 'Drive on, please!'

The carriage sprang into motion. The ride was bumpy over the rough grass and body- jarring tree roots, but Ruby was thankful she did not need to walk any further. 'What an unusual way to travel. What happened to the fast car?'

Morganite stroked the intricate gold leaf detail imprinted in the carriage door. 'It is quite spectacular, don't you think? I have travelled this way from Little Love Forest. That is my true home. In Little Love Forest, it is all about love and romance—even their means of travel. I mean, is this not the most romantic way to travel?'

Ruby nodded. They were silent for the remainder of the trip. Ruby drank in the scenery and enjoyed the weight off her feet as they cantered towards Little Love Forest. At first impression, it was as one might expect—a myriad trees of all shapes, sizes and colours. Every tree had red and white hearts hanging from its branches. Ruby reached out to touch one nestled amongst the trees. A stream filled with the bluest water ran through the area of the forest where they parked. Several hundred lanterns with candles inside floated down the stream. Corked bottles floated in between the lanterns, holding tiny scrolls of paper tucked inside them. Ruby was intrigued.

'Come along, Ruby, we really need to get your ankle looked at,' Morganite said. He offered Ruby his hand as she stepped out of the carriage, then helped her to a hut made of bamboo with a thatched roof. The room contained a bed with starched white sheets. There were bundles of lighted candles on shelves, flickering and providing a warm glow. There were freshly cut flowers in vases on top of two teak vanity units with louvre doors.

A woman dressed in white entered the room. Her long dark hair touched the base of her spine as she walked as if reminding her of its existence. She carried a hand-woven basket of medical supplies. She had a wide smile and perfect white teeth. She started to wash and dress Ruby's foot being careful not to push or prod too much. When she had finished, she said, 'Rest now,' and left the room.

Ruby lay for a short while contemplating her adventures. She pulled her Ruby from her pocket to check that it had also survived the black ice lake ordeal unscathed. Her ankle started to feel much better and the swelling reduced almost immediately after being treated. She noticed there were Lotus flowers in the potions and appreciated the part they must have played in her ankle's miraculous recovery. Her head met the soft plush pillow and her eyelids began to drop. She slowly floated off to sleep. The sound of a peaceful bubbling stream being the last thing she remembered.

She heard a tap on the door. Morganite had returned. He had brought fresh fruit. They sat for a while focused on eating the fruit. 'Would you like a walk into the village?' he asked.

Ruby looked at her ankle. She thought she should be able to walk on it for a short time and would like to see Little Love Forest. 'Yes, please. That would be great.' Morganite opened the door and led Ruby out of the hut. There were many huts side by side and sheltered by the trees. Morganite and Ruby walked over a rickety, well-trodden bridge. There were people all around— some standing outside their huts, others walking the streets, some on rusty old bicycles. All looked cheerful and in high spirits. The most obvious thing about Little Love Forest is that most people were in couples, strolling hand in hand, laughing, kissing or talking. There were endless displays of affection and total adoration. Ruby understood why her mother had fallen in love in such a hypnotic place. Ruby herself felt seduced by its beauty and the emotional draw of love and contentment.

They walked the full circle and returned to the hut she had first visited. Morganite decided she had probably had enough of an introduction to Little Love Forest and that she should get some more rest.

'I will leave you in peace now. If you need anything, I am in the hut immediately facing yours. If you are unable to walk, just shout.'

Ruby thanked Morganite and returned to her room. She saw several books on the bookcase and decided to read. She took a book onto the balcony and sat on a wooden bench that looked to have been built into the balcony of the house. She could hear the feint noise of crickets outside. She took a candle and placed it on the arm of the bench. After reading two chapters of a romantic novel, she placed the book on the floor.

Ruby thought it might be nice to walk to the stream and see the lanterns in the moonlight. She threw a shawl around her shoulders and sauntered into the cobblestone street. The stream was not too far from the hut. When she reached it, there were other people gathered around the water's edge, placing lanterns or bottles into the water. She wondered, *what do the bottles represent and what is in them?*

She heard a male voice from behind her. 'They are love wishes. Whether people are single or in a relationship, they travel great distances to the Stream of Undying Love to place their love wishes into a bottle and allow it to float down the stream. The common belief is that whatever you wish for will come true.'

She turned on her heel to see a young man with dark, shoulder-length curly hair and green eyes. She was immediately struck by how handsome he was.

'Well, that is certainly different from my last visit. My previous adventure involved a lake of black ice and some strange-looking dark creatures.'

A smile crossed his plump lips. 'I see. That would be Ice Valley. The creatures are called Dark Shadows. They belong to Whitney the Sable Witch. I am surprised you did not see her. She would have been there. The Dark Shadows are mostly blind. They rely on sound and take their instructions from Whitney.'

Ruby's ice lake experience started to make sense. It had been clear they could not see her. The only confusing part had been when they turned on her after she reached the other side. They must have been given an instruction by Whitney.

'You were lucky to survive it. They are vicious and merciless creatures.'

Ruby nodded. She wholeheartedly agreed with the young man's assessment. 'I am Ruby,' she said.

'I am Daylin,' he replied. They shook hands politely as if they were afraid to break each other. 'If you would like to learn more about the forest, I would be happy to show you,' he said. Ruby's teeth began to chatter with the cold, and she decided it would probably be best to return to her room, just in case she was missed.

'Maybe tomorrow,' she replied. 'Would that be okay?'

Daylin nodded. 'Okay with me. I will walk you back to your hut, so I know exactly where to find you in the morning.'

Ruby thought this quite gentlemanly. They walked the short distance back to her hut. The sky now black except for a sprinkling of stars which had muscled their way to the surface providing a little glamour to the night sky. The surrounding huts had their shutters firmly shut. It was as though everyone was asleep in their beds. The pathway to the hut was quiet, and people had disappeared from the streets.

When they reached her door, Daylin leant forward close to her cheek and whispered, 'I will be back in the morning.' Ruby smiled and walked up the wooden steps onto her balcony, then through the door to her room. She closed it gently behind her. She put her back against the door and stayed there for a moment. She felt light and carefree all at the same time. Ruby looked forward to tomorrow and spending time with

Daylin, but now she must join all the other inhabitants of Little Love Forest and get some sleep.

The following morning, she found more scrumptious fresh fruit in her room. She opened the wardrobe to find something different, she could wear today. She still wore the rags she had been provided at Rat Pits. She found mostly summer dresses, many of which would fit. She thought they might have been Morganite's. He would not mind if she borrowed one. She selected a white cotton simple A-line dress with a V-neck and a bow at the back. This was plain and unfussy, and it should keep her cool as Little Love Island seemed to have a warm climate. There was a free-standing bath filled with water stood at the foot of her bed. *Someone must have prepared this especially for me* she thought. She could not recall if it had been filled last night, but she had succumbed to tiredness over cleanliness. She stepped into the bath, which smelled like rose petals. She did not want to take too much time, as it might be embarrassing if Daylin were to arrive early. She must get ready.

She dried quickly with a grey towel that she took from the dresser and started to put the dress on. She became trapped for a moment in its bodice when she almost put her head through the opening meant for her arm. She was all a dither. She did not know why she was so nervous. She heard a tap on the door, so she rushed to open it. Morganite stood in the hallway.

'You look beautiful. Are you ready for a walk?' he asked.

Ruby looked a little sheepish. 'Morganite would it be okay if I walked with a friend I met last night?'

Morganite looked horrified. 'What friend? I left you in your room!' Ruby could see the disappointment in Morganites face.

'I am sorry, I went for a walk down to the Stream of Undying Love and made a friend. His name is Daylin. He told me about how people send their love wishes up the stream and that they come true!'

Morganite clapped his hands over his face.

'Oh, dear, not that old story. I grant the wishes, Ruby. I collect as many of them as I can each evening and spend my nights making wishes happen. Tell me, did Daylin touch you?'

Ruby thought back. 'Yes, he shook my hand.'

Morganite slapped his hands on his face, this time with even more force.

'Then, it is done. The reason Daylin was at the stream was to plant his own wish. A wish to fall in love with the next girl he chose to touch, and that girl was you. I promised your mother I would not leave you unescorted after what happened to her. I am in so much trouble!'

Ruby was shocked at his outburst and did not know if she believed all this love wishes business.

'Morganite, please calm down. This is not your fault. Who said anything about love? Daylin is my friend?'

They were then interrupted by a second knock on the door. Morganite opened it without looking to see who it was and bowed as if allowing Ruby to leave. Ruby stroked Morganite's cheek on the way past. 'Everything will be fine, I promise,' she said.

Weeks rolled by and Ruby and Daylin became inseparable. They went on long walks in the forest. They took bikes sometimes and made picnics full of sumptuous food in their favourite clearing. Some evenings they watched the ritual of the Stream of Undying Love. They learned all about each other. Daylin was a woodcutter's son who lived in the forest. He had grown up in Little Love Forest and had not ventured farther. His father was old now and relied on him to help ensure there was enough wood for the villagers to make their huts and fires. His mother passed away many years earlier, but she was in his heart every day.

Morganite did not really spend any time with the couple. Occasionally, he would eat with them just to check they were okay. He did not want to get in the way. They would sometimes cook for Morganite to say thank you for his hospitality. In the evenings, they would drink wine and sit next to a roaring fire talking about every topic they could think of—favourite music, flowers, foods and even magic. Daylin was not born into a White Witch family, but he was part of a White Witch community, so he understood a little about it and the White Witch rules. He knew his village had been protected by the White Witches in the past, and his family had been grateful for that.

It was quickly becoming obvious to everyone that the two were undeniably in love and this worried Morganite because he knew that the day would come when Ruby must depart. He was surprised it had not happened yet. One evening they were walking across the cranky old bridge when they heard the patter of water in the distance. Ruby did not notice at first.

Daylin said, 'My goodness, rain. That is rare in Little Love Forest.'

Ruby jumped. 'Run!' she shouted. Daylin thought it best not to argue with her, as she was already dragging his hand. They ran as fast as they could, not stopping for breath until they reached Ruby's hut. Panting they collapsed in a heap on the balcony.

Daylin shook his head and looked puzzled. 'What in Validor was that all about?'

Ruby started to breathe more evenly. She explained what she had learned at Professor Clapton's house. Daylin listened intently and when she explained it a look of relief cast over his chiseled features. *Thank goodness I did not try to stop her* he thought.

'Wow, that is the saddest thing I have ever heard. Well, at least some good came from it. We were saved from the same heartbreak.' He then scrambled up from the floor and kissed Ruby's forehead. 'That is enough excitement for one day, I will catch you on the morrow.'

Ruby kissed his hand and watched him walk away, his strong athletic frame disappearing into the distance and at that moment Ruby knew she loved him. Every time she looked at him, her stomach lifted, and her breath became short. She could not imagine a life without him. She began to feel somewhat fatigued. She removed her dress and lay it on the dresser and put on her linen nightdress. She lay down and watched the rain fall onto the path outside her door. It's sound rhythmic and musical. Then she drifted off to sleep.

She had only been asleep for a moment when the sound of tapping woke her up. At first, she thought it was rain, but the tapping got louder and more insistent.

She wanted to ignore it, as she was still drowsy. She lifted her head up to look through the glass. It was Morganite. She pulled down her nightdress, which had been crumpled beneath her as she slept and walked to the door.

Morganite stepped in. His face looked grave. Ruby had a bad feeling. 'What is it?' Morganite knew that Ruby would be wounded by the news and wanted to find the words to soften the blow.

'Is it Daylin?' Ruby sat on the bed; her eyes totally focused on what Morganite might say next.

'Say it, please.'

'He came to my home last night, he wanted to know if the White Witch Coven would allow him to marry you.'

Ruby looked astonished. She had thought for a second he had come to some harm, but this—well, this was the best news she had heard for a long time. She felt her heart rise and pound in her chest. Daylin felt it too. He loved her. She could not think of anything she would want more at that moment than to marry Daylin.

'Morganite, he makes me so happy. He brings such love and joy into my life with each second we spend together and...'

Before she could finish, Morganite held his hand in the air. 'Ruby, I am so sorry. You cannot marry Daylin. You can only marry someone who has White Witch parentage. Daylin does not.' Ruby fell back onto the bed. Her heart sank. Why had she not known this? 'That is why I was supposed to escort you around the village. To fall in love is okay. Everyone who visits

Little Love Forrest falls in love. That is why it is so popular. However, a White Witch must marry into a White Witch family to protect the bloodline. If you do not, you will lose your powers, and any child you might have would have diluted powers or none. We must grow the White Witch family to protect the world from Sable Witches' evil. Do you understand?'

Ruby understood. The tears streamed down her face now. 'It just seems so unfair,' she stammered.

Morganite held her close. 'You will find love again. I cannot promise it will be as pure as that which you have with Daylin, but it will happen,' he said, stroking Ruby's hair.

'Is there no way?' Ruby asked.

Morganite shook his head. 'The only person in the White Witch community who can choose anyone they wish to marry, White Witch parentage or otherwise, is the White Witch queen. The reason for this is because a White Witch queen is given much more powerful magic, which means she would have the power to pass on magic either to her husband or children, and it would remain strong.'

Ruby was not a white queen, so she knew that Daylin and she could never be together. Morganite straightened the shoulders on Ruby's nightdress. 'Now, I am afraid you must leave Little Love Forest. The White Witch Coven believes it is best for both of you, and you must go now.'

Ruby looked at Morganite with a pained expression on her face. She blew her nose with a handkerchief that had been sitting next to her bedside unused. She shook her head, shrugged her shoulders, held her hands in the air in a posture of surrender and said, 'Okay.' She did not have the energy to fight the witches. If she could not have Daylin, then she would prefer to go now. That way, she would not have to see his beautiful face every day and long to be close to him.

Morganite patted her back. 'Good girl. You are a strong young lady. Remember, you have the love of your family. They will help you through your sorrow. We all must make sacrifices sometimes. This one is for the greater good. So long as the family's strength and bloodline remain, we can keep our world from the Sable Witches. Gather your cloak, and I will take you to somewhere where it will be easier to forget.'

'Where am I to go next?' Ruby managed to say in a choked voice and still battling back the tears and losing. Her throat began to hurt. 'You will go to Wisdom Dome, Ruby.'

## 25

# Wisdom Dome

Ruby's heart was heavy-as if it were full of the world's tears. She thought it might break with the burden of her sadness. She knew she must go. She wanted to say goodbye to Daylin but feared if she did she might never leave.

Morganite ushered her to the carriage. He was still in his dressing-gown but elegant as ever. It was made of the finest silk with embroidered edges. It was little compensation to be taking a trip in something familiar this time, even though she would travel by the light of the moon.

Morganite placed his arms around Ruby. 'The White Witch community will never forget the sacrifice you made. I will make sure of it.' He lifted her chin so that she could witness the sincerity in his eyes. Ruby smiled as best she could and lifted the hem of her nightdress and scaled the wooden steps into the carriage. She heard Morganite speak with the driver but could not make out words. It sounded like a low mumble. She did not have the inclination to listen harder because she felt so drained and listless.

The carriage shook into motion. It rocked from side to side, almost tipping on occasion when it met with rocks in the path. The air was still. They sat in almost complete silence except for the sound of the horses' hooves clip-clopping on the path. Sometimes loud, other times unobtrusive. She tried to sleep, but her mind would not settle.

Ruby thought of Daylin and how he would react when he learned she had gone. She knew Morganite would make sure he got through his heartbreak, but what distressed her most was the thought of him falling in love with someone else. She could not bear it, so she pushed the thought from her mind and replaced it with a song. She made sure to choose a song whose words were difficult to recite.

Ruby had been singing the words without interruption for a short while and did not notice the carriage had ground to a halt. Her eyes were shut, as it helped with her concentration. She came to the last few words of her song and opened her eyes. It was still dark, and they were no longer moving. She could hear the horses snorting as if they were clearing their nostrils. She thought perhaps the driver had took a break. It seemed like a good idea. Perhaps a stretch of her legs outside the carriage would make her feel fresher. She opened the door and stepped down carefully. She did not want to lose her footing in the dark, although the moon did provide a stream of silver light, so it wasn't completely dark. It was like a shimmering silver penny in the night sky.

She looked at it in awe, then out of nowhere came two boys. They were dressed in shorts and tee-shirts with bandanas across their noses and mouth. Their clothes were encrusted with dirt and sand. She jumped and let out the smallest scream. Why were they not home in bed at this late hour?

One of the boys stepped forward. 'Give me your shoes,' he said with a snarling mouth.

Ruby felt her heartbeat to pick up speed, the fear rising in her chest as her breathing quickened at the same rate. The boy was next to her now, stepping around her, looking her up and down. He was so close she could feel his breath on the back of her neck as he walked behind her. Her body shuddered. *Who were they, and what did they want?* She looked at the driver's bench. He still wasn't there. The palms of her hands began to sweat, and her mouth became dry.

'Okay, I will give you my shoes, but you need to give me some space to take them off,' she replied assertively. She did not want the boy to hear the fear in her voice.

He pushed his forehead against hers and said, 'Very well,' then he took two steps back. She sat on the steps of the carriage and removed her shoes. The boy ripped them from her hands. 'I can sell these,' he said to the other boy. Then before she could blink, the driver appeared from behind some bushes and pushed the two boys to the ground. The boy who had the shoes threw them as far as he could while lying flat on his front. The driver grabbed them both by their tee-shirt collars. They tried to escape, but the driver overpowered them.

'Now, I could really hurt you, or you can come with us peacefully and help Ruby on her journey to Wisdom Dome. Which is it to be?'

The boys knew they were beat and did not want the man to hurt them. 'We will help you, as long as you promise you will not hurt us, and you will let us go when we get there.'

The driver nodded. 'Good. Agreed. Now, I need you to draw a map in the soil that shows how to get to Wisdom Dome. I only stopped the carriage because I thought we were lost.

The boys pulled a stick from the bushes and started to sketch the route to Wisdom Dome on the ground. It was not far away, and it did not look like a complicated route. They would need to pass through a tropical forest but there were no other landmarks.

The driver pushed the boys up the steps and into the carriage. One of them banged his head on the doorway on the way through. Although Ruby was grateful to be safe, she still had no shoes! Once they were all safely in the carriage, the mares sprang into action in their usual dependable way. Ruby huddled into the corner of the carriage; not entirely comfortable with sharing it with two strangers, especially as they had stolen her shoes. They seemed to have resigned themselves to taking the trip and were both sitting on the opposite side of the carriage at either end of the seat.

Their eyes were fixed firmly on the outside as if trying to avoid any conversation with Ruby.

The boys smelt like they had not bathed for some time. She could see cuts on their legs that looked like bramble marks, thin red barbed wire shaped imprints on their shins. She thought they might be homeless and living on the street. She held the Ruby in her hand, as she knew that this would help build a friendship between them. A few hours passed, and the carriage stopped. This time Ruby noticed instantly. She stepped out of the carriage, and the boys followed. The driver dropped down from his bench.

'We are at the mouth of the tropical forest. I cannot take you any farther than this, as the carriage will not make it through such boggy land.' Ruby looked at the land beneath the tall, lean green palm trees. Although it was covered in white Orchids, it was also saturated by water. She feared the driver had been right. The carriage would not make it through the tropical forest, but how would she, especially without shoes?

She did not want to make the driver feel responsible for her, so she thanked him, gave the horses a stroke and a thank you and watched them ride back down the same path they had just travelled. She watched them until they were only a speck on the horizon. The boys were still dutifully at her side; they remembered the promise they had made.

Ruby took a long breath and placed her feet into the sludge. It felt cold and slimy between her stub like toes. Each foot sank at least four inches every time she took a step, and she made slurpy sounds when she lifted a foot out of the mud. She looked up into the palm tree canopy. She hoped it would not rain, as that would make things so much more unbearable. When she looked up, she noticed movement amongst the shiny spiky leaves and was surprised to see brown and squirrel-like monkeys with flashes of white fur that ran from the centre of their heads down their backs, but their most stunning feature had to be their eyes. They were wide and brown, almost human-like.

One of the boys spoke. 'These are Tamarin monkeys.'

Ruby stared at them. Totally captivated by their unusual looks. 'How lovely they are,' she said.

One of the monkeys shimmied down the tree and landed on the mud next to her feet, then another and another. One leapt over to Ruby and grabbed her right hand. The others grabbed the boys' hands. Before they knew what was happening, the monkeys dragged them up a palm tree, dangling them by their arms. Ruby felt her arm would fall off as the monkeys leapt at full speed, from tree to tree as though they had been carrying humans this way all their lives.

The views from the treetops were spectacular. They passed frogs and ants which appeared decidedly uninterested in the new visitors to the forest. Little time had passed when Ruby could see something shining straight ahead. It looked to be a giant snow shaker in the middle of the tropical forest. It was a perfect dome shape. She knew this had to be Wisdom Dome. She breathed a sigh of relief as they neared its entrance. The dome reached into the sky, and it looked palatial. It had walls of glass, and she could see inside it. It looked as though parts of the forest were trapped in the dome yet still enjoying the sun and their usual surroundings with the added protection of a glass shield.

They reached the foot of the dome. The monkeys let go of their arms and disappeared back into the forest. They crumbled to the ground in a very undignified landing. Ruby's arm had started to ache, so she started to bend and flex it, hoping that might help. The boys were doing the same and rolling their heads around as if they had cricked their necks during their monkey adventure. They had completed their side of the bargain and were about to make their way back through the forest, except this time on foot, when part of the glass wall slid to one side.

Ruby had not noticed a doorway; it had magically appeared. Sapphire stood on the other side. She looked fantastic. She wore a white gown dusted with tiny blue Sapphires and a gold headband with a diamond-shaped sapphire in the centre. Her magnificent onyx black locks cascaded onto her shoulders complimenting her beautiful dark skin. She was a vision. It made Ruby feel ashamed at her own appearance. She was still wearing a nightdress and no shoes!

Sapphire greeted Ruby with a cheery hello. She placed her arms around her waist and gave her a squeeze, almost lifting Ruby from the floor as she did. Ruby gasped for breath.

'Sapphire, wow, you look terrific!' Sapphire laughed and completed a model-like twirl showing of each angle of her dress.

'Ruby, you look, well, not good,' she said, looking her up and down. Ruby laughed; she was grateful for Sapphire's honesty.

'Who are your friends?' Sapphire said, pointing to the boys who had started to walk towards the trees. The boys had not wanted to make conversation, so Ruby had not forced it. She did not know their names.

'Hey!' Ruby shouted. The boys were still in hearing range. 'What are your names?'

One of the boys shouted back. 'I'm Peter, and this is Luke.'

Sapphire bellowed out, 'Come in, guys. There's plenty of food for all and a warm bath.'

Peter and Luke stopped in their tracks and looked at each other. Food and a bath sounded like music to their ears, and there was no real reason to rush back. Yelling, 'Thanks', they headed back towards the door.

Once they were all inside, the door slid shut behind them. It was as though it was never there.

'Keeps the bad guys out,' Sapphire said, answering the unspoken question. They walked along a corridor with a midnight blue floor. The walls were all glass. Everything in the dome in glass or crystal. They found themselves in a room at the centre of the dome. It had a seating area and a kitchenette.

Sapphire pulled out one of the six glass seats from around the round glass table and gestured for Ruby to be seated.

'Boys, come with me,' she said. She took them through one of the side doors then returned moments later. 'I thought I would let them take a bath and give us some time to catch up!'

Sapphire took a glass mug from one of the glass cupboards and filled it with something from a glass kettle. It looked like a hot drink with cream on the top.

She placed it in front of Ruby on the table and Ruby began to drink it. The drink tasted like nectar. Ruby could feel her energy returning with every sip of the hot sweet liquid. It warmed her feet like a cosy set of your favourite wooly winter socks. Ruby started to tell Sapphire about her trip so far. Talking about all her adventures and trials helped Ruby to unburden some of the more difficult parts. At the end of the conversation, she felt lighter. Sapphire was a good listener and fascinated by all that had happened since she last visited with Ruby.

'What an extraordinary story. You have learned so much already. I am so glad I can play my part in your learning. I really hope you like Wisdom Dome.'

Ruby did not get a chance to reply, as the boys had now returned. They looked like different people, and their bath seemed to soften their expressions. Sapphire stood up.

'Sit down, boys. I have as much food as you can eat,' She shouted, 'Join us monkeys,' and several of the little monkeys they had seen in the forest appeared. There were trays and trays of vegetables, fruit, fish, cheese, bread and cakes. Ruby had never seen so much food. The monkeys joined them in their meal, they were part of Sapphire's family. They ate in silence for a while. They were all ravenous and could not cram the food into their mouths quickly enough. Sapphire finished first, and then broke the silence.

'I am so excited to show you all the secrets of the Wisdom Dome. Boys, you can treat this as your home for as long as you like. The only thing I ask is that you do not follow us into the rooms that we enter. Have fun!'

Sapphire and Ruby rose from the table at the same time, and Sapphire led Ruby out of the room. As they entered the next room, the glass surrounding them misted. Now no one outside the room or the dome could witness Sapphire's magic. The room had a large glass round table on a single pedestal. The table was at waist-height, and inside it an ornate clock face. In the centre of the clock face, a place showing the day, date and year. Sapphire explained that this table gave people special gifts. The gifts were so special that even the people around them did not realise they had been fortuned with White Witch magic, only that they were different somehow. Sapphire set the date to today's date and placed her sapphire in the holder inside the clock face.

'Watch,' she encouraged Ruby. The sapphire shone brightly, and the clock face turned into something that resembled a round television screen. Inside it, she could see a couple who were in a maternity ward. They gazed adoringly at their new baby. 'This is a special child, Ruby. It will be different from any other child as it will be bestowed with gifts that cannot be matched by any other.'

Sapphire reset the calendar to ten years later. Ruby could see the screen and the images looked to be on fast forward, and then they stopped and began moving at a normal pace. She could see the parents from the maternity ward. They looked older but were smiling at their child. Sapphire said, "They are teaching their child at home. This child could not be taught in any regular school. He had different learning needs. Teachers were baffled with his extraordinary skills.'

Ruby continued to watch the scene. The parents were playing a game with the child. They were placing cards down one by one, and the child mathematically added one to the next. There must have been a hundred cards in the pack, but the child could add each one to the previous one without effort and in seconds.

'He has wisdom like no other, Ruby. Not everyone gets a child like this,' Sapphire narrated.

Ruby had never seen such skill in her own classroom at school. This is pure genius. *His parents must be so proud*, Ruby thought.

Sapphire continued, 'Did you know that Albert Einstein, Amadeus Mozart and Charles Darwin were some of the many people with similar extraordinary gifts? In the human world, they would say a child has learning difficulties. In the White Witch world, we would say the child has a splash of awesome!

• • •

Sapphire took her hands off the table and made her way to the door. 'I have more to show you,' she said. They went into a different but near identical room. The walls misted. Sapphire went through the ritual she had performed in the previous room once again. The sapphire gleamed with magic. Sapphire placed her hand on the screen, and it revealed a different scene— a girl struggling to read, sitting with a teacher. The scene changed to the same child being taught to write, but it was impossible. The child could not read or write. The teachers tried but eventually gave up on her. Again, the parents began schooling her from home.

Sapphire leaned forward and changed the calendar, this time to thirty years in the future. Ruby investigated the screen and recognized the face of the child, now a woman. 'We give these children special gifts for a purpose. The child who had not been able read or write became a famous artist. Others who we bless with this gift become athletes, attorneys, or actors and join so many other professions.' Ruby learned so much from Sapphire. Sapphire said, 'They are our visionaries! They have such a unique perspective on the world.'

They left the room and moved into the next. Although each room appeared the same, an entirely different story was revealed which showed the magic of the Sapphire in all its glory. On the third table, Ruby could see a child who was in a classroom, surrounded by other students completing their work at their desks. All were focused on their work, except for one. He was charging around the classroom with boundless energy. He frequently left the classroom and returned, still racing around the desks.

Sapphire reset the calendar to ten years in the future. The same child now in a hospital trauma room, responding to an emergency. Saving people's lives every day. 'Their gifts are incredible, and their contribution to this world is phenomenal. They do things differently, but never underestimate their abilities,' Sapphire said in a low and serious tone. 'One more room,' she said encouragingly, leading the way as she spoke.

On the table in the final room, Ruby saw a distressing scene. A child had run into the road, and a bus had knocked her down and rolled on top of her. The sapphire started to light up inside the clock, and at the same time, the mother arrived at the scene. The mother walked over to the bus and lifted the bus! Ruby could not believe what she had witnessed.

'Is that real?' she asked.

'Yes. These are tiny pieces of magic miracles,' said Sapphire with a wink. They stayed in the last room for a short while longer. Sapphire wanted to show her one more scene. This time she saw a child on a playground who did not quite fit in with the other children. The other children played around him, and he neither tried to join, nor was he asked to play. It was unclear from the scene why this might be, but as Sapphire used her magic to move time forward, they saw how this child became a principal dancer in the ballet *Swan Lake*. He travelled all over the world, and people travelled all over the world to see him.

Sapphire explained. 'It does not matter who you are, what you are, where you came from, or what you look or act like. You are an important person to everyone—yourself, your family, your friends and everyone you meet. We all have so much to offer, so much life to live. We are all truly incredible. We must grab life and all that it offers. It will be a blast, and who knows when White Witch magic is being worked on you behind the scenes?'

Ruby felt moved by the whole experience. She felt enlightened and wise from Sapphire's teachings. Sapphire slapped her on the back, which startled Ruby. 'Come on, my dear, I will show you your room.'

They returned to the central sitting room. The boys were laughing between themselves and feeding some rather large fish in a tank that extended from the floor of the dome to the ceiling. They were laughing because the fish were grinning and pulling faces at them, and the boys were in competition with the fish trying to see who could make the silliest shape with their faces. The women passed through, smiling at their antics. Sapphire opened the door to Ruby's bedroom. In it were a glass bed and wardrobe and some glass shelves on the wall.

Darkness fell outside. Ruby sat down on the bed, and Sapphire left the room. The stars shone through the ceiling of her bedroom. She thought it might be a good opportunity to send a message to her mother. She took out the ruby and pointed it to the sky, carefully spelling out each letter. 'Having a great time with Sapphire at the Wisdom Dome. Looking forward to seeing you soon. Love, Ruby x. She smiled smugly. This was quite an achievement. She had successfully sent her first White Witch message!

She lay down on the shiny blue bedding. The lights, which were tiny round circles in each part of the glass, went off. She imagined there must be a sensor that meant if she stopped moving the lights would turn off. As she wallowed in the silence of her bedroom. She thought it might be a good time to allow herself a few kind thoughts for Daylin. She wondered if he would be at the stream or walking the streets and if Morganite was looking after him. A wave of grief passed over her. She missed Daylin. She had welcomed the distractions but would much rather be in his arms.

Ruby tried to erase the thought but struggled; even a complicated song did not do the trick this time.

She heard a strange hooting noise. It sounded like three owls, all hooting in slightly different pitches. She saw them flying toward the window of her bedroom, the window that had manifested as magically as each door did. As they flew closer, she could see their feathers were brown with white and red flecks. Their eyes were piercing blue, as blue as the ocean. Their wings were splayed and elegantly carving their way through the night sky.

They flew through Ruby's window and rested on the glass windowsill. It looked to be the perfect place to grip with their claws. She felt sure they had done this before. One of them started to speak to the others.

'Did you see that? First I was like, swoosh, then I was woosh, then I was eeeeee, down into the window.'

Another spoke 'Totally radical, dude, I was like, wooo.'

The third said, 'Hit my nose on a dragonfly, I think. Totally decks.'

Ruby tried to hold back a laugh. They were like a comedy act. One hit the other with a wing as if reminding him where they were. He responded by clearing his throat and speaking as though he was reading from a script.

'Oh, yeah. We came to give you the last important message for your learning while you are in the Wisdom Dome.'

Ruby tried not to giggle. 'Really, thank you. I am honoured.'

The owls continued their speech. 'I am Mizaru. I see no evil.'

'I am Kikazaru. I hear no evil.'

'I am Iwazru. I speak no evil.'

They each took a turn introducing themselves. Ruby allowed them to continue uninterrupted this time.

'Our message to you is simple. If you try to live life in a way that sees only good, hears only good and speaks only good, this will be a great kindness to all who are blessed by your company. Try to see the good in the people that you meet. Give them the benefit of the doubt. When they speak, seek the goodness in their words and whatever you witness people doing, try to understand that there may be some good behind it.'

Ruby thought this was so profound that she was at a loss for words. She would take this advice and carry it with her each day and check that she was staying true to the owls' advice. 'Thank you, wise owls, I am forever in your debt.'

They patted one another on the back as if saying, well done.

They were ready to leave her bedroom when Ruby said, 'One last thing.' They settled again to listen to her final words. 'Totally awesome flying!' They all laughed and flew off into the darkness.

Ruby decided she would love a bath. She noticed a side door in her bedroom, which led to a bathroom. She would take a long hot bubble bath and get some sleep.

## 26

# The Battle of Mystic Moors

Shortly after Ruby had left Blankinsa Caves, King Organza came to his senses. Once Ruby left the caves, Organza snapped out of the White Witch spell. He looked around trying to recall what had happened. He remembered a struggle between him and Ruby and nothing much more after that. He looked around the cave. The spiders were still there, and his trusted spider, Spinaka, was at his side.

'Where is she?' he bellowed into Spinaka's face, spitting as he did. Spinaka began to shake.

'You, you told me to show her the way out, your majesty, I only did as I was asked,' he stammered.

King Organza's face turned purple with fury. 'You fool! She put a spell on me, and you watched as she did it!' He paced from side to side, looking at the floor as if trying to think of a plan. He pushed his face close to Spinaka's eyes this time. 'You got us into this mess, now you will make sure we get out of it. Ruby must not succeed in her mission. It only strengthens the magic of the White Witch Coven. Get Whitney.'

Spinaka sped away, muttering to himself that it had not been his fault. Some hours later he returned with Whitney. She was skinny with grey hair which reached her feet. She wore a black dress covered in real icicles that never melted as her flesh was typically at sub-zero temperature. King Organza came to the balcony at the top of the stairs where he had first greeted Ruby.

'Whitney, you came!' he said in an ingratiating way.

'Cut the niceties, King Organza. I know you want something from me,' Whitney replied.

Organza smiled slyly. 'Yes, my spies tell me you also failed to get rid of our unwanted visitor. They tell me your clumsy Dark Shadows let her slip through their claws.'

Whitney rolled her eyes. She was bored now. 'Organza, what do you want? Insults will not help you.'

Organza looked defeated. 'Okay, okay. I need your help to make a last attempt to get rid of Ruby.'

Whitney was interested. 'Go on,' she said.

Organza started to pace again as he explained his plan, 'She will soon be crossing Mystic Moors; I say we provide a horrible welcome party. One they will never forget,' Organza said before he broke into a long dark cackle that seemed to start in his stomach and reach his throat. Whitney started to cackle in an ugly way too. The only thing they had in common was the enjoyment they took in thwarting the White Witches.

Unknown to both witches, they had been over-heard by Solomon, who sat on one of the gantries above them. Solomon liked Ruby; she had helped save his life. He knew he must get word to her. He sneaked out of the cave room and made his way to the cave exit. He raced across the volcanic ash as fast as his legs would carry him. He felt sure if he could at least get word to the dragon, the message would eventu-ally reach Ruby. *However, how could he get the dragon's attention!* The only way he knew was to get into the stream. The thought terrified him. What if the dragon did not come in time? He found a long thin tree root and pulled it from the ground. He tied one end to an adjacent tree and the other around his chunky spider body. He walked back to the stream and stepped in with his eyes shut.

He really hoped he lived to tell the tale. He kept his eyes scrunched tightly shut and waited and waited. His body shook with cold, and he nearly gave up until he saw the dragon coming from the distance. He breathed a sigh of relief. Today was not his day to die.

When Nodrog arrived, he looked confused. He could see that Solomon was not really in trouble and safely secured to a tree. He turned his head to one side as if trying to work it all out.

'Nodrog, I am sorry I had to do this to get your attention. It is Ruby, you see. She is in real danger. The Sable Witches are taking an army of spiders and Dark Shadows to greet her on Mystic Moors. I need you to get a message to her.'

Nodrog understood. He pulled Solomon out of the water and swiftly lifted his wings and flew into the night. Nodrog knew he needed to find White Witch Emerald. Emerald was the only White Witch with psychic ability, and as Nodrog could not speak, he needed someone who understood him. Emerald lived at the White Witch Coven. She was the gatekeeper. She protected the White Witch Coven making sure someone is always home and that all visitors to the coven had good intentions.

Nodrog became thirsty, so dropped to the ground to drink some fresh water from a stream he had seen whilst he had been flying. He would take a drink, then fly over to the White Witch Coven. As he drank, he heard a rustling behind him. He turned his head carefully around to find Emerald walking through the long corn behind him.

'Do not be surprised, Nodrog. I am psychic, remember? I know when someone needs me. I just need to get closer to pick up your message clearly. It is hazy from the Coven. Damn signal!'

She stood next to Nodrog, stroking his head and concentrating on reading the message. It was obvious when it had properly reached her, as she fell backwards onto the ground, landing on her bottom. 'Oh no, poor Ruby!' she said.

She pulled out her emerald and began to form a message in the stars. That was the best she could do, as she needed to get back to keep watch on the Coven. 'Thank you, Nodrog. You did well.' She clicked her fingers and opened her hand. In it was his favourite treat—gumballs. She placed them in his mouth and disappeared into the corn again.

Sapphire burst into Ruby's bedroom. 'Are you awake? I have just read such terrible news.'

Ruby had drifted off to sleep, but she awoke abruptly with all the commotion. 'What is it? What happened?' She had never seen Sapphire so rattled.

'King Organza and Whitney are sending an army of spiders and Dark Shadows to Mystic Moors.'

Ruby frowned. 'Okay. So, what does that have to do with us?'

Sapphire swallowed hard, finding it difficult to tell Ruby the news because she had continuously tried to nurture a positive state of mind in Ruby.

'Please don't panic, but tomorrow you must cross Mystic Moors.'

Ruby sat upright in the bed 'What? How? I mean, is there no other way?'

Sapphire shook her head. 'I am afraid there is not.'

Ruby started to hyperventilate. She remembered the Dark Shadows well, with their hockey masks and black fur capes. 'Well, what can we do?'

Sapphire began to think. They did not have an army. They had never needed to battle. 'I think we could use some help, Ruby. I will call on Alexandrite. He can empower and strengthen. I think we could use that somehow. He is not far away; he usually stays at Pearl's house in Compassion Crystal Mountain. I think he still hopes she will forgive him someday.' Sapphire leaned out of the window with her Sapphire and created a message for Alexandrite in the stars.

Alexandrite and Pearl were having a glass of witches' brew on a garden seat, reminiscing about their childhood together, when they saw the message in the stars. Pearl looked at Alexandrite.

'You must go.' Alexandrite knew she was right, but this was a battle. This was not a White Witch thing. Not for centuries. They were the peacemakers of Validor. 'What if I do not come back?' he whispered.

Pearl's eyes glazed over. She could not bear the thought of losing Alexandrite, but she did not want him to see that. She played with the thread in her long white linen dress. Pearl was known to be an unemotional sort of character, and she did not want Alex to see her vulnerability. 'That is not the attitude to have, Alex, White Witches do not do failure. You will go to this battle and win, and I will see you tomorrow night. Now, do not be too long. You know I get bored.'

She turned on her heel and walked back into the house. She did not want him to get a glimpse of what she was truly thinking or feeling. She had work to do. If she could find the right blend of magic, she could use it to influence some parts of the battle remotely.

Alex left Pearl's house, climbed into his car and made his way to Sapphire's. When he arrived, Ruby and Sapphire were pleased to see him. Sapphire rushed towards him and gave him a light kiss on the cheek. 'Boy, are we pleased to see you.'

Alex held his head high with pride. *There can be no doubt I am the hero today* he thought. It was not often he got the chance. He wished it had been a less precarious set of circumstances but was glad to do his part.

'So, what defense do we have?' he asked.

Sapphire shrugged, 'The only defense we have is you, me, Ruby, Peter and Luke, some monkeys and some owls.'

Alex shook his head. 'How many monkeys?'

Sapphire had never counted. 'Maybe a hundred or so?' she replied.

'And owls? How many?'

Ruby and Sapphire answered together. 'Three.'

Alex could see they had limited options. 'We need to round up the monkeys in the forest, the boys and the owls. Can you do that?'

Sapphire anxiously paced the room energised by adrenaline and keen to help.

'Yes, of course.'

Alex clasped his hands together. He meant business.

'Great. Leave the rest to me.'

Sapphire disappeared and returned almost an hour later. Ruby and Alex had made themselves at home in the kitchen area. They both had strawberry milkshakes and were drinking them when Sapphire returned.

'I have them all,' she announced. 'They are waiting in the forest.'

Alex stood up and walked towards the front door of the house. 'Excellent. Let's get to it,' he said.

They left the house together and walked down the forest path. They could hear the chatter of the monkeys. Occasionally, they heard a quiet hoot amongst the crowd of monkey chitchat. The monkeys rarely gathered this way, so they knew something important must be taking place.

Alex coughed and waved his hands in the air as if pushing the noise of the voices down to the ground.

'Hi, my friends. I am Alex. I really need your help. There is an army of Dark Shadows on its way to Mystic Moors as we speak. Their mission is to get rid of our student White Witch, Ruby.'

The monkeys started to talk amongst themselves, with a general tone of outrage. Alex knew he needed to speak over them to settle the chatter. 'You are the only army we have. Violence is not the White Witch way, so where we can, we settle this battle with intellect and compassion.' He pulled the Alexandrite stone from his pocket. 'I will pass this stone to the first monkey on the front row. He or she should pass it on so that each of you holds it in the palm of your hand. When the stone reaches the last monkey, please return it to me.' The chattering began again. 'My friends, please, let me finish. This stone carries my magic. For the period you are close to me during the battle, you will be empowered. You will be able to achieve anything your heart desires. Use it wisely.'

Alex walked to the front row of the monkeys and passed his alexandrite stone to the first monkey. It took a while for it to cross the hands of all the monkeys, but it eventually made its way safely back to Alex.

Sapphire stepped forward. 'Thank you, my kind friends. I will never forget what you have done for us this night. If you ever need anything, you only need to ask. Tomorrow we leave for Mystic Moors, and I know that if I have you all beside me, all will be well.'

There were a few hours of darkness left, so they all returned to their beds to get some much-needed sleep. Tomorrow would be a long day.

When Ruby awoke the next morning to a house bustling with activity. Sapphire, Alex, Peter and Luke were in the kitchen preparing a hearty breakfast and some snacks for the trip.

'Hi Ruby,' they all said in chorus. Ruby could see they were all trying to make her feel relaxed and was grateful for the gesture.

'How do we travel to Mystic Moors?' asked Ruby.

Alex answered first. 'We spent some time strategizing last night while you were asleep, and we think horses will be best. The monkeys will not have experienced riding on horseback, but as I have empowered them, they will be able to ride with minimal effort.'

Ruby looked a little put out. She would have liked to join the strategy meeting.

'Why horses? What will we take with us?' she said, eager to catch up with the plan.

Alex had a mouthful of toast, so Sapphire answered.

'As the spiders will be on the ground, and the Dark Shadows are unable to see properly, the horses will disorientate them somewhat. We will make sure the monkeys have body armour as we do not know if they will bring weapons. The trick is to remember we are only trying to get you safely across Mystic Moors. We must all get home in one piece.'

Peter came into the kitchen from the front of the house.

'The horses and monkeys are ready. Yours are waiting outside.'

They all put down their food and drink and followed him to the front of the house. The monkeys looked like something to be reckoned with, all in matching body armour and on horses. They were excited to be part of this important part of Validor history.

Alex mounted his horse and rode to the front.

'Let's go!' he said, and they all cantered off across the fields next to the rain forest.

The dust from the horses formed a cloud behind them. Ruby rode at the back for her safety, as Sapphire had instructed. They rode for around three hours and were all feeling sore.

Alex signalled them to stop and take a break. The monkeys sat on the floor and removed their helmets to get some air. They were wearing full-face masks, and they were all in danger of overheating and dehydrating. The boys had brought bottles of water in saddlebags and were passing them out. They all drank every drop, not knowing when they would get the opportunity to drink again.

Alex mounted his horse and gestured to the others to do the same. The monkeys all pushed their helmets back on and joined him. They started with a trot, then changed into a fast canter. They felt strong and ready for the battle. The ride was mostly flat and over fields. After around an hour, they knew they were close because the temperature had dropped, and the air was frosty. A thick fog had dropped, making visibility almost impossible. They could see just enough through the swirling fog to make out the Dark Shadows, and the spiders looked to be low down on the ground behind them. Both armies were headed straight for each other, neither with any intention of quitting.

The mass and the movement of the two armies together in such a tiny space made the earth shake. They were now almost touching, and the monkeys were using their batons to push away anything that got in their path. The Dark Shadows were not running in the same direction; some ran left, others right, some straight ahead. Noise from the horses' hooves and their whinnying had knocked their senses out of kilter. The spiders were trying to avoid being trampled on and dodging this way and that. The Dark Shadows had spears and were lashing out at nothing most of the time, as they had lost the use of their personal navigation systems. Occasionally, one would get a lucky shot at one of the monkeys, but before they were able to land the spear, an owl would fly down and take the spear from them.

It was total chaos—horses braying, owls hooting, monkeys chattering, spiders shrieking and the Dark Shadows stumbling. If it was not so serious, it would have made for good comedy. Peter and Luke were playing their part too. They were off their horses and playing hopscotch on the spider's backs which was totally infuriating the arachnids. The monkeys began showing off with their new monkey magic and were leapfrogging across each other from horse to horse. Sometimes they made jumps that took them over four horses. They were shaking one another's hands each time they made a successful dare devil leap while continuing to bash the spiders and Dark Shadows with their sticks.

Just as it had all started to become a bit of a joke for Alex's side, Whitney and King Organza appeared from the back. They had spears and were wafting them from side to side in the hope whatever the spear met would be injured or maimed. Sapphire rode forward; now, to take her turn.

Whitney and Organza separated. Whitney rode around the back of Ruby and gripped Ruby around the throat.

Sapphire shouted 'No!' and the whole battle came to a standstill. Sapphire spoke calmly and quietly now. 'Let go of her, Whitney. If you harm her, you will never be able to use your magic again.'

Whitney laughed. 'Idle threats. Let me guess. This is one of your pathetic prophecies?' Whitney was looking at Organza now. 'What will you have me do, King Organza?' she asked.

Then, to everyone's surprise, Morganite appeared. 'I would ask your friend to let her go, Organza if you know what is good for you.'

King Organza spun around to face Morganite. 'Well, well, well, if it is not my goody-two-shoes little brother.'

Everyone on the battlefield gasped. Nobody had known that Morganite and King Organza were brothers. Morganite stayed focused on keeping Ruby safe.

'You stopped being my brother the day you chose to go to the dark side, Organza. You failed at the tests to become Queen, but you were so determined to have a crown, you chose to be a terrible person. You are not and will never be part of my family.'

Organza was hurt by Morganite's words but tried to hide it. Morganite knew that somewhere locked away in Organza was a desire to be a part of the family again; he had just become greedy. 'If you give the instruction to Whitney to drop the spear, I might forgive you. But if you don't, I will disown you and banish you from our family forever.'

Before Organza could react, one of the owls swooped down and took away Whitney's spear. She jumped in the air trying to retrieve it, and because of the distraction, Ruby managed to uncouple herself from her grasp.

Alex cantered through and scooped Ruby off the ground and threw her face down over the back of his horse. The monkeys formed a protective circle around Alex and Ruby, and they pushed their way through the remaining Dark Shadows and spiders. Morganite followed Alex and his army across the moors. He turned and shouted back, 'You should have done the right thing while you could, Organza.'

Once they had all safely crossed the Mystic Moors and the fog had lifted, Alex let out a victory cheer, shaking his fist in the air. They all cheered with him. Even the owls gave one another owl high-fives. The only two who were not cheering were Peter and Luke, who looked completely traumatized by the whole event. Now that it was over and the adrenaline levels had dropped, they realised the seriousness of what had just happened on the battlefield. They could have been killed. They nearly lost Ruby.

Sapphire took charge this time. 'Come on, boys. Let's get you to Healing Island. We must first pass White Swan lake and camp for the night.' She turned to the monkeys. 'Monkeys, you are so brave. We could not have done this without you. Now you must return home to safety. We will be okay. Thank you all.' The monkeys took off their helmets as if to tip their caps at Sapphire, Alex and Ruby, then turned their horses around and trundled back through the Mystic Moors. There was no sign of the spiders or Dark Shadows as they were no longer interested in the monkeys. Ruby was their target, and the Sable Witches had failed miserably.

# 27

# Healing Island

After all the excitement, Alex, Ruby, Peter and Luke thought a little calm was needed. They gently trotted south towards white Swan Lake. They felt the pace needed to slow down a little to give everyone time to digest what had just happened. Sapphire came with them for the initial mile, then once she felt sure they were on the right track, she gave them a huge hug goodbye and started the long journey back to Wisdom Dome.

Peter had not spoken since they left the battle-field, and Luke anxiously checked behind them every few minutes, convinced they might be followed. The horses were also tired. They had worked so hard through the battle, and now they faced some hills as they faithfully carried their precious cargo. Alex tried to come to terms with the whole night's events. He wanted to remember every miniscule detail for Pearl. He knew she would want the whole story.

Ruby spoke first. 'Is this White Swan Lake?' she asked Alex. They were in front of a large lake of green water, slowly rippling powered only by a breath of wind. On its surface were ten elegant swans gliding across the glass-like surface of the lake. Their feathers were pure and white, seemingly untainted with life and the dirt of Validor. There were three signets who looked to be staying close to their mothers as if fearing any unforeseen predators.

Alex slid off his horse and adjusted his clothes around his legs. His pants had started to bite into his skin, and this had been a tad uncomfortable.

'Yes, this is White Swan Lake,' Alex replied. Everyone dismounted their horses in an unsophisticated and sloppy way. They all had lost any scrap of finesse they might have had with horse riding. They were exhausted.

'We should go no further. We will camp here this evening,' Alex said in the style of their battle leader. He found it difficult to step back out of character and felt that he was the leader of the party.

Luke pushed himself between Ruby and Alex. He grabbed Ruby's and Alex's arms and pulled them down to speak into their ears. He nervously looked around, then whispered, 'Do you think it is safe to stay here? I mean, it is so open, they might come. There will be spiders all over us, and those things, those Dark Shadows, well, they will burn our eyes out with their lasers. They will probably eat us. I bet they haven't eaten for days!'

Luke's mind had become a horror film in his imagination and one that he could not stop. Now totally convinced they were in danger. Alex looked at Ruby. Luke had become fragile after the battle, and he worried about him.

'It is okay, Luke. I'm here. Morganite has returned home, but if King Organza tries to harm us, he would be back in a heartbeat. Luke did not look convinced, and Peter seemed even more sullen.

'Do you see the swans on the lake?' Alex said.

'Yes,' replied Luke. 'Well, those swans have a swan forcefield. Anything that comes within one mile of us without good intentions, the swans' forcefield will protect us.'

Luke dropped his tense shoulders. 'They are lovely creatures, aren't they, I feel safe now. Would you mind if I lay down? I am really tired.' Luke yawned.

Ruby glanced at Luke and half smiled. Pleased that he had relaxed. She cleared some dried leaves from the ground to make a space for her cloak, which was wide enough for Luke and Peter to lay on.

'Here you are,' she said. They lay down instantly and went to sleep. The darkness began to creep in, but the moon shone brightly reflecting in the lake. The swans clearly visible, dancing gracefully on the lake.

Ruby leaned on Alex. They were both facing the lake, sitting upright alongside each other on the grass. 'Alex, how strong is this swan forcefield? Would it help against a Sable Witch?' Ruby asked. She knew the boys were asleep.

Alex pulled a blade of grass from the ground and began to chew on it. 'There is no forcefield, Ruby. It was merely a white lie to make the boys feel better.'

Ruby was shocked. She did not like lies, even little ones. She thumped him gently in the shoulder and gave him a disapproving look.

Alex half-smiled. 'It worked, didn't it?' he said, not really expecting an answer. 'Luke is like the swans right now, Ruby. They look to be gliding along effortlessly, easily even through life, but underneath their legs are frantically paddling, driven by fear, especially the little ones. They are afraid of what might come next, who might attack them, when they might eat, if they can swim. Even swans suffer from anxiety, Ruby. You just don't see it.'

Ruby thought it was a great analogy. 'And Peter, is he a swan?'

Alex shook his head. 'No, Peter is not the swan. If he were, he would be the swan sat at the lakeside. The swan that had decided it is all too much, that life is just too hard, and his legs cannot paddle anymore. There would be no way he could swim, even if he tried. He has given up.'

Ruby thought *this is awful* 'Do you think it was the battle that made them this way?'

Alex placed his hand on her arm to reassure her and said, 'No, do not blame yourself. The battle will not have helped, but the boys had a hard life. They were homeless and stealing so that they could eat. Who knows what led to the life they were living? The combination of all those things will not have helped.' Alex lay down on the grass with his hands behind his head.

'The only way we can help now is to reach Healing Island. Pearl will know how to help them.'

Ruby lay down herself and allowed herself to fall asleep

Ruby and Alex had to wake the boys in the morning. Peter refused to move at first, saying he was too tired and did not want to go anywhere. Alex insisted he get up at least to give Ruby her cloak back. Peter reluctantly stood up. The others mounted their horses.

'Are you coming, or should we just leave you here? You will be cold and hungry,' Alex said to cajole Peter into getting onto his horse. The boy did not respond, but he did climb onto his horse. He remained at the back throughout the journey, moving as slowly as they would allow him.

They rode all through the day without stopping. Alex decided stopping might be unwise. He needed to get the boys some help, and he knew that Healing Island is a day away from White Swan Lake. They needed to travel the entire northern boundary which separated the realms of the White Witches and Sable Witches. They would pass Little Love Forest but did not have time to stop.

Ruby could see the coast stretched out in front of her like a sprawling mass of diamonds shining in the sunlight. They were close to the border now. She hoped Alexandrite had a plan to get them from the coast to the island. Before she could ask, three fairies landed right beside them. She remembered how a fairy had carried her from Hope Coast.

Alex began to explain. 'Fairy Gardens is close by. The fairies are a community by themselves. They do not belong to the White or Sable Witches, but they rarely cause problems, unlike the Pixies. They often help with a sort of taxi service. All they ask in return is help from the White Witches should Fairy Gardens ever face any trouble. Works for everyone.' He shrugged. 'There is only one condition. They will only travel in their own locality, which is why we cannot use them on the other side of Validor.'

The fairies latched themselves onto Ruby, Alex, Peter and Luke's clothing and took flight across the sea of diamonds headed for Healing Island. Pearl had been waiting, standing in her garden with her legs apart and her hands on her hips. Her body language showed her growing impatience. The fairies dropped the travellers one by one at Pearl's feet in an uncoordinated landing. Their legs were a tangled at first, but they managed to pull themselves apart. Peter and Luke were particularly unhappy about the journey and were dusting the sand off their pants.

'Welcome,' Pearl said with her head slightly bowed. 'I am honoured that you have chosen to visit me. Please come this way.' She walked towards a large square platform made from flat square boulders pushed together to make a kind of boulder jigsaw puzzle. Over the top of the rocks a canopy covered with traditional Chinese carvings could be seen. The canopy looked like a temple roof, tiered and curved and pointing high into the sky as if receiving important spiritual messages. Seated around the edge of the plinth were monks. They looked silent in meditation and were all sitting cross-legged. At the back of the room was a stone table and in the centre of it, a complete oyster shell. Ruby could not see inside, but she knew this had to be Pearl's pearl.

Pearl sat on the floor and encouraged the others to do the same. Ruby looked around the room. She noticed Opal; she winked and smiled at Ruby, not wanting to interrupt Pearl. Opal was seated on the ground helping some of the monks (using her magic, of course) paint pictures onto large canvas blinds. Pearl had asked Opal if she would help decorate the blinds that she used to protect them from the wind during meditation. On each blind were paintings of the precious jewels. Opal's masterpieces were nearly complete. Ruby had never encountered such a calming and spiritual place.

Pearl went behind the stone table and produced fresh fruit and water. She started to place plates of fruit on the floor next to where her guests were seated. They were grateful for this and began to eat. Pearl allowed them to finish and begin speaking when they felt they were able.

Peter spoke first 'It was horrible. I keep having nightmares about the spiders' beady red eyes. I am afraid to sleep, and I cannot get rid of the thoughts in my head.' Pearl nodded sympathetically.

Luke spoke next. 'I don't feel safe anymore. I do not think they are done yet, and I keep looking around, expecting them to turn up.'

Pearl nodded again. Then she said, 'Why do you choose to call these images to your mind? This is only causing you suffering. Life is hard enough, and your own thoughts are hurting you. If you like, I can teach you both how to stop those thoughts and to choose different thoughts. You probably think that is impossible, but I promise with the right training, I can show you how easy it is. Would you like to try?' she asked gently.

The boys looked at each other. They both wanted to be free of their worries and anxieties, free from these thoughts that were torturing them and stopping them from enjoying their lives. They realised Pearl was right. They were the ones placing the thoughts in their heads, so if they had put them there, then they could get rid of them too.

Pearl removed the food dishes from the floor and asked the boys to sit with their legs crossed, hands open in their lap and their eyes slightly open (so that they did not fall asleep). She began to speak in a calming tone and guide them into a meditation that would help clear their minds to create space for some more positive thoughts. First, they focused on their breathing, then on emptiness. Pearl asked them to think of all the things they could be grateful for in their lives, of all the people they would like to send positive thoughts to who may need their help.

Ruby struggled at first to wrestle out the random thoughts that came into her head, but sometimes she did manage to think of nothing. She realised how powerful this exercise was. By teaching her mind not to think of anything but her breathing or gratitude or others, if she was ever having more negative thoughts, she would do the same. *What a wondrous gift Pearl had given to them all.*

Even after a short time, the boys looked calm and refreshed. They began to smile again and talk more casually. They did not look as fraught with worry, anxiety and stress as they had when they first left the battlefield. The meditations went on for several days. Pearl told them that when they made their minds quiet and empty. That will receive important messages. One day, Pearl took them for a walk to Compassion Crystal Mountain. A place where Pearl met with some of the monks to find ways to help the people of Validor. A mountain with a cave at the base filled with crystals—agate, angelite, quartz and jasper, to name a few. Together the monks and Pearl would sit and contemplate ways to help people who were suffering. She wanted to teach the boys that to be selfless and to help others was one of the ways that they could experience true happiness and that buying themselves things or having expensive holidays and cars would never make them feel truly fulfilled. If they truly wanted to be contented and fulfilled, they should give to others. It need not be material, just their time, a kind smile or positive words would often be enough to make a difference to a person's life.

The boys helped at Compassion Crystal Mountain every day, even if only to clean or talk to anyone who visited. They enjoyed their time there so much they did not want to leave. Ruby decided to show that she had been a good student with Pearl. She decided that she needed to be selfless.

'Pearl, please do not feel obliged, but Peter and Luke have had a difficult life and never really had anywhere they could call home. Although I need them to help me on my travels, it would be best for them if they could live here in Compassion Crystal Mountain. I know this is a lot to ask, so please do not feel obliged.'

Pearl bowed her head, just as she had when they had first arrived. It was a humbling stance. 'It would be my pleasure to share my home and mountain with Peter and Luke. What a blessing they are.'

Ruby thanked Pearl. She knew in her heart that this was meant for the boys. This was a great kindness she could offer them, and she had learned that kindness was the best medicine you can give.

The time came for them to leave Healing Island. Alex wanted to stay with Pearl, as they were still secretly in love with each other but not ready to face it. Ruby thought one day she would take them to Little Love Forest, as that might help move things along. Alex, Pearl, Opal, Peter and Luke walked with Ruby back to the beach.

'Thank you all. I will miss you,' Ruby said.

Luke laughed. 'You won't miss us; we are coming with you!' Ruby knew they only wanted to help, but it would be best for them both to stay with Pearl.

'Thank you for your kindness, but Pearl and the monks of Compassion Crystal Mountain could really use your help.' Luke and Peter looked at Pearl.

'If you would not mind staying, that is?' Pearl said. The boys grinned from ear to ear. They finally felt they had a home and a family. They started to chase each other and play fight while Ruby, Alex, Opal and Pearl said their final goodbyes.

## 28

# The Moon of Validor

Ruby watched her friends make their way back to the house. Ruby was standing on the beach trying to work out where she would visit next. She turned and shouted to the group. 'How will I know what to do next?'

Opal turned to face her and yelled, 'When the sun and moon touch the sea, the path will become clear!'

Ruby appeared put off by the answer. *Why did some people like to talk in riddles instead of plain English?* She thought.

She knew that she must wait and hopefully all would become clear. It was a breathtaking vision when the sun started to slip into the water from above. The kind of sunset picture that everyone has in their holiday collection. Ruby found herself questioning why most people were so moved by the sun as it made its daily descent beyond the line of the sea. Was it the combination of blue water and red and orange flashes of colour in the sky? It was nature's masterpiece that everyone had bought.

The sun bounced lightly on the waves, then started to drop beneath them, or so it would seem. The sun and moon of Validor were not like the sun and moon on earth. You may recall the sun and moon were a single planet made of half fire and half moonrock. When the fire side of the planet faced Validor daylight came, and when the moon side faced it, it was night. Watching the sun rotate into a moon is a spectacular event. Nowhere else on earth could such an image be seen. Ruby was quite content to sit and watch it. She was transfixed by this miracle of Validor. The sun had now moved to half rotation. The moon was fully visible. It was night. Then, right before her eyes, the sea parted, revealing a pathway which was solid underfoot. In an instant, Opal's words made sense. The sun and moon had touched the sea, and the path did become clear.

Ruby started to walk up the path, taking half steps. Her stomach turned over and over- 'OH!'

She exclaimed at this magnificent magical sight but felt a tiny bit terrified. After what felt like a lifetime, she had reached the end of the path. She saw a large golden gate. On one side of the gate was a picture of a sun and on the other a picture of a moon. On the sun side, there appeared to be a button for a bell in the middle of the sun. She needed to get close enough to push the bell, so she walked to the left. She placed both hands on the button. It was a huge button, larger than both hands. She used all her might to push the button as hard as she could. Nothing happened. She pushed it again and still nothing. Then she heard pattering paws on the ground. There seemed to be many paws headed her way, getting closer and closer. A chorus of barks echoed through the air. It was a crowd of dogs. Fortunately, they were behind the gate, which still had not opened. She counted; there were nine. They looked like husky dogs and handsome ones at that. They had black fur coats with white faces and feet. Their eyes were a distinctive bright blue colour. As you looked into the dog's eyes, you were sure they could see inside your soul. The started to quiet down when they heard someone rushing towards the gate on their side.

It was Moonstone. Her red hair was sticking out all over her head as though she had just woken up. She had a large white bow wrapped around her head and rollers were sticking out from under it. She looked strange, but that is what Moonstone is, but everyone loved her for it. She wore a sheep shaped onesie with bulky fluffy sling back slippers on her feet.

'Okay, guys, okay. I hear you, I am coming,' she yelled, still trying to run and almost losing her slippers in the process. She got to the gate.

'Oh, Ruby, it's you! No one mentioned you would be arriving. My goodness, what must I look like?' Ruby felt awkward for arriving unannounced, but she had not known how to let Moonstone know she would visit. She had not known herself until a short while ago.

'I am sorry., I tried to ring the bell, but I do not think it works.' Moonstone was adjusting her hair. 'Oh, it rang' she said, 'but only the dogs can hear it. It is one of those high-pitched things, you know it goes eeeeeeeeeeeee.'

Ruby put her hands over her ears as the sound Moonstone made was so loud. She tried to shout over her. 'Okay, I understand. You can stop now!'

Moonstone smiled. 'Okay, let me try the key,' she said, drawing a gold key the size of her arm from her pajamas. She tried to jam it into the gate in the area where the moon was. There was a tiny hole in the moon ornament, but it was not large enough to fit the key in. Moonstone stopped for a moment and scratched her head. Then she tossed the key to one side and said, 'I don't really need this. I was just playing with you. Open gates,' she commanded, and the gates swung open.

Ruby smiled. This was going to be a fantastically interesting and fun visit! Then she remembered the dogs. 'Are they tame?' she asked.

Moonstone nodded. 'For you, yes. They are trained to protect the White Witches. Come inside. I will make us a banana whizz bang milkshake,' she said.

They walked up the metal grilled path together. She could see a large modern house. It was white and on stilts in the shape of a spaceship, or what you might expect one to look like. The door was an eye. As they approached it, the eyelid opened, and the pupil could be seen.

'Retina identified,' a robotic voice said.

*What a remarkable security arrangement.* Ruby thought. As Ruby was with Moonstone, she was able to tail gate and walk in behind her, but just as she did, a cage dropped down onto Ruby and a green laser light passed over her.

'Visitor has no concealed weapons,' the robotic voice spoke again. The cage lifted, and Ruby was released. Moonstone smiled.

'Thank you, Third Eye. Sorry, Ruby. It's just doing its job,' she said apologetically. They were in a corridor filled with wires and machinery now, and a lift shaft could be seen running up the middle of the building. Moonstone called the lift. 'Third Eye send the lift please,' Moonstone said.

'Lift dispatched,' replied the robot. The lift doors opened, and they both stepped inside. Once the doors were closed, the lift moved at a super-fast pace. Ruby felt her cheeks pushed to the side of her head with the centrifugal force the lift speed had created. Even if she had wanted to speak, it would have been impossible. They reached their destination, and the doors opened.

Moonstone stepped out first. They were in the centre of the spaceship house. It was a dimly lit room with modern black décor. At the back of the room was an open plan kitchen area with few utensils or cooking instruments on show. Everywhere was clean and new looking. A pristine and uncluttered place. In the middle of the room was a stone circular fire pit. Ruby could see flames licking the side of the stone where a fire had already been lit and looked to be trying to escape.

Moonstone said, 'Please, sit, relax,' as she pointed at the leather sofa curved around the firepit. Moonstone began to prepare their milkshakes in the kitchen. The room was dark except for the light of the fire and some sparkling kitchen lights hidden beneath the cupboard units. The milkshake was delicious, thick banana-flavoured with cream, and Ruby drank it in almost one gulp. As soon as the glass became empty, the straw shot into the air and exploded like a firework. It was spectacular.

'Whizz bang?' Ruby asked.

Moonstone smiled 'Never get bored of it!'

'I disagree. The banana is the best,' Moonstone said.

Ruby was confused, she had not spoken.

'Excuse me, I did not speak, and I really would not know.'

Moonstone said, 'Get serious, the strawberry is definitely over-rated.'

Ruby was really puzzled now.

'Okay, Moonstone, my weirdness monitors just reached a new state of alert. What are you talking about?'

Moonstone laughed. 'I was talking to the others,' she said, waving her hand in the air.

Ruby looked around her. There was nobody there.

'Are you okay, Moonstone? There is nobody here but us.' Ruby said in a concerned voice.

Moonstone slurped the last bit of her milkshake, and her straw whizz banged through the air. She winked at Ruby.

'Are you sure? Look again.'

Ruby looked around, more slowly this time. Then she noticed a handful of lights floating around the room. They were tiny specks.

'What are they?' she whispered, just in case they could hear her.

'They are people. This is how we start life and how we end life. If they pass over, they sometimes hang around to help their loved ones, or if they have not been born yet, they visit me just to pass the time mostly. They are great fun. They like jokes if you know any?'

'That is amazing,' Ruby said.

Holding an emotionless expression on her face so Moonstone would not see she was skeptical.

Moonstone smiled. 'I am never lonely. They are all my friends. I get down sometimes when they leave for their new destinations, but I am pleased for them, too.'

'Sylvia is here you know'

'Grandma is here, where?'

'She says not to worry and that everything will be fine. She has your back'

Ruby had a confused and pained expression.

'Don't worry. She has gone now. She did not want to scare you only to give you comfort'

Ruby began to tap her fingers nervously on the table.

'So, only people who are no longer with us and those waiting to be born?'

'I help the new life. As you know, that is my magical power. Using my moonstone, I can ask a new life to go to couples who would like a baby. That is my favourite thing in the world to do. I feel sure I might do it for you one day but only with a new moon. My powers are at their strongest then.'

Ruby thought this had to be the coolest thing she had ever heard. Except for the bit about her having a child, of course. She was a long way away from being ready for that.

Moonstone continued to talk with the lights. 'You are a funny girl. The chicken jokes are getting old,' she said.

Ruby wondered how she could hear them. 'So, do we become lights at the end of our lives? I know we can live for hundreds of years, but when we do pass over, what happens?'

'Well, we are peculiar, because for short periods White Witches can transform into the white lights. We can only do it using a powerful meditation technique that Pearl teaches us. We only transform into the light when we visit the White Witch Coven together. We do this because we do not want anyone to know that all the White Witches are in one place together. If the Sable Witches were to find out, they might plan an attack on the Coven or Validor as it would be left without White Witch protection.'

Ruby thought this was a genius plan. 'I would really like to experience that someday,' she said. Moonstone leaned forward and kissed her on the forehead.

'It will be sooner than you think, my love. You have come to the end of your learning; this is the penultimate stop. You will be visiting the White Witch Coven soon. The last step in your training.'

Ruby could not believe she had finally reached the end of her induction.

'Wow, I have really finished!' she said, feeling so very proud of herself.

'Well, not quite, Ruby. The White Witch Coven has its own challenges, but I know you will do well!'

Ruby looked in wonder into the flames, then at the tiny lights floating around their heads. She could never have imagined such a life as the one she had.

## 29

# The White Witches' Coven

Moonstone and Ruby stayed awake most of the night drinking milkshake after milkshake and laughing and talking until they were too tired to carry on. They were both excited about what was to come tomorrow. She learned they would have the pleasure of visits from all the White Witches. They would all sit together, much as Moonstone and Ruby were right now, and begin a collective meditation. It was an important session. If they were successful, they would all become a tiny ray of light for a short time—time enough to allow them to travel safely to the White Witch Coven, visit and return. Ruby would finally find out if she had passed all the tests required to become a true White Witch.

They said their goodnights to each other and the white lights and made their way to Moonstone's bedroom. Moonstone liked her guests to share her bedroom with her. It resembled a large dormitory with several beds in it. Each witch had their own bed. Moonstone loved to spend time with the witches and never liked to miss a moment when they visited. They would tell each other stories of Validor, eat chocolate and watch films. Moonstone looked forward to every visit. It was such fun. Tonight, she would let Ruby sleep as she needed to keep her strength up for the visit to the White Witch Coven.

Both Ruby and Moonstone slept through the entire day. Even hunger did not wake them. They must have needed the extra hours. They were embarrassed when they awoke to see all the White Witches (all except Morganite) gathered around their beds.

Moonstone bolted upright in her bed. 'What? What time is it? How did you all get in?' Ruby began to stir and opened her eyes. She almost leapt from her bed when she saw the party that had gathered in Moonstone's bedroom.

Sapphire laughed her loud, unmistakably raucous laugh. 'Girl, you must have been done in. Third Eye recognised us, and after a laser search, let us come in.'

Moonstone began to get dressed. She pulled on white leggings a leotard and a white tutu. Sapphire looked at the other witches, expecting someone to make a remark about Moonstone's choice of dress, but they were all used to her being eccentric so said nothing.

'I am so hungry,' she said.

232

'Me too,' said Ruby in a croaky, half-asleep voice.

Pearl had already left to prepare food. They all started to walk to the main room in an orderly line. The fire had died, and there was no sign of the other floating lights. 'It is a bit chilly in here,' Pearl said. She was furiously chopping raw vegetables in the kitchen on the other side of the room. She clapped her hands together and blew into them, much as Morganite had on Ruby's visit to Hope Coast. This time the fire flashed through Pearl's hand and fired across the whole length of the room and into the fire pit, narrowly missing Moonstone's unkempt hair. The fire came to life with a roar.

Moonstone was convinced her hair was on fire too and was furiously patting it. It seemed frazzled and smoking, but she was not on fire. Moonstone gave Pearl a glare.

Pearl shrugged and said, 'Sorry.' The witches helped Pearl place the plates of food on the leather sofa, and they all began to eat. When they were all finished, they returned the plates to the kitchen.

'Please, push back the sofa and be seated on the floor. Make yourselves comfortable,' Pearl said. She wanted to start the meditation. They pushed back the sofa, took off their shoes and placed them against the walls of the room.

'Let the games begin,' Moonstone joked. Pearl gave her a stern glare. She took the meditation seriously; she did not want to leave anyone behind and had to make sure they were returned safely to their current form. The slightest mistake could mean the end of all the

White Witches. This was a serious matter, and Pearl was a serious individual!

They all closed their eyes and Pearl began to whisper the magic words

'Lightania Menanca Portaya.' After she said the words, the witch to her left must repeat it, then the person to their left until everyone had repeated it. This exercise was repeated five times. On the fifth occasion, each witch popped into the air in a puff of smoke. Out of the fire flew new balls of light; each ball of light was one of the White Witches. They were all floating above the fire pit.

Ruby said, 'It worked. It worked!' She found herself trying to look for hands or feet, but she no longer had any.

Pearl took charge. 'Before we fly, does anyone know where Morganite is?' The others hadn't noticed he was missing.

'No,' they answered together.

Pearl said, 'Okay. Well, we must go. We cannot wait. We do not know where he is or how long he will be, and I do not want to keep Queen Diamond waiting. Follow me. No messing around and stay close. Did you hear that, Moonstone?' Pearl asked. She knew Moonstone could be wild at times, but it was all in the name of fun.

'Yes, ma'am,' said Moonstone, intimating that Pearl had become like a schoolmarm. Then Moonstone shouted, 'Last one there is a crunchy carrot!'

They all laughed and joined in the race. Even Pearl raced, but not before giving Moonstone the obligatory disapproving stare! Ducking and weaving between each other, it was a spectacular sight, almost like the Northern Lights. They darted amongst each other, trying to overtake or slow each other down. Ruby felt exhilarated, flying faster than a bird in the night sky. They were invincible like shooting stars!'

'Here,' said Pearl. Ruby looked shocked and disappointed that the journey was over. It was like the best fairground ride you could ever go on.

They were floating in front of a white mediaeval-looking castle. The gardens to the front of the castle were well established. There were large flower beds and shrubs crammed into every spare space. *There must be a keen gardener close by*, thought Ruby. It was a garden that could win competitions. She could see the gateway to the castle. It was not a traditional gate. It was a large stone doorway with an arched top, and the doorway itself looked as if it were filled with wavering ripples of light. You could not see behind it, yet it gave the impression you could push your hand through it as though it was air.

Pearl said, 'We need to wait until the forcefield clears.'

They paused for a second and the shimmering gate disappeared, leaving an open stone archway. 'Not going to be a crunchy carrot,' shouted Moonstone, and she flew ahead, determined to win the race she had started. The others followed. They were in a courtyard covered with large stones. It was difficult to make out in the darkness, but on closer inspection, Ruby could see the stones were the colours of the nine precious jewels, repeated across the floor over and over. The courtyard had a secure wall around it, and there were four stories, each with a balcony that overlooked the courtyard. The balconies had archways and behind the arches were many doors. On the ground floor stood a line of guards all in white armour. They were all standing in the same stance. They surrounded the whole perimeter of the courtyard

'White Knights. They are the queen's guards,' whispered Opal into Ruby's ear.

• • •

'Please be silent! Queen Diamond is on her way,' one of the knights shouted.

Piano music played in the background a gentle but uplifting melody. The talking stopped and a clicking noise could be heard getting closer and closer to the courtyard. Queen Diamond came into view, leaning on a long silver staff as she walked. She had a white dress on which shone with a thousand diamonds stitched into its fabric. The train of the dress at least five feet long behind her. Her hair long and silver. Half was pinned to the top of her head, the other half rested on her back. At the sides of her hair were diamond brooches. Her face old but fresh looking and showed a lifetime of great wisdom and kindness. It was obvious a very special being had entered the courtyard and in that instant, you knew why she had been chosen as Queen.

'Greetings, my angels,' she said. 'It has been a long time since we have met this way, and I am so pleased to have you visit. This will be the 50th ceremony I have conducted as the Queen of the White Witches, and I never tire of its significance. I am eternally proud when a witch matriculates and becomes all that she can be and joins our fight for good. However, we must not get ahead of ourselves. There is one more test that Ruby must pass in order to succeed. By this time tomorrow, you must be able to recite all the magic that lies in each of the precious jewels. You have been shown a brief glimpse of the extent of each jewel's powers. You must now study the remaining ones. You will be tested in the morning. To help you, you can take your White Witch family into the library. If you fail tomorrow, you can return to your mother, but the Ruby will remain at the Witch Coven until someone worthy of its gifts is found. Do you have any questions?'

Ruby understood what was required but felt fearful that she might not pass the test. She wanted to be part of the White Witch family so badly and to bring good things to the world and Validor.

Moonstone squeezed her arm. 'I would still be your friend with or without the Ruby,' she said reassuringly. Ruby squeezed Moonstone's arm back.

Queen Diamond turned around, clicking her staff on the floor as she did. She was about to walk away when she turned her head to look back. 'No Morganite, I see. Tell him his absence is noted' Then she took the slow walk back into the archway.

Ruby did not want to waste any more time and asked Pearl to lead her to the library. They floated up the corridor and up to level two. She saw the sign for the library. Ruby gasped, astounded by the array of books. There must have been thousands—shelf, after shelf, after shelf. She was overwhelmed.

'I do not know where to start,' Ruby said.

Sapphire stepped in. 'Most of the books are recorded moments in Witch history. Moments where White Witches used their powers against dark forces. You do not need to be concerned with this. In the main, you just need one book. Sapphire pulled a large red leather-bound book from the case. This was a strange sight as the book was glowing in her grip. The book had gold lettering on it. *The Secret Magic of the Nine Precious Jewels*. She dropped it on the desk next to Ruby. 'Our work is done. Come on, girls,' she said. 'Time to play tricks on the White Knights again.' Ruby began to protest, but they had already disappeared.

Ruby read each page by candlelight rubbing her eyes continuously. It was the only thing she could do to stay awake. Her eyes wanted to close, but she fought it. She felt she had not learned nearly enough. She wanted to make her mother and Grandma Sylvia proud and strengthen the name of their family. The words had started to become hazy and had stopped making sense some time ago. She realised her brain had just about as much as it could handle this evening. If she did not know it now, she never would. She decided to wait in the courtyard. She would not sleep for fear of losing all the information in her head. She lay on the cool stones and shut her eyes and waited.

She must have fallen asleep because when she sat up, the courtyard balconies were now filled with people. The only people on the courtyard itself were the White Knights, Queen Diamond and Ruby. A buzz of excitement filled the air.

Queen Diamond cleared her throat. 'Let us begin. When I shout the name of a jewel, you must first run to the correct colour stone in the courtyard and shout out all the magic each one carries. Are you ready?'

Ruby did not feel ready, but it was now or never. She took a breath and nodded. Pearl had been asked to be the scribe. She stood in ready to record the results.

• • •

'Opal' said Queen Diamond in a loud and firm voice.

Ruby panicked for a moment. Her eyes raced across the courtyard stones to find the Opal. She found it in seconds, but it felt like a hundred years. Then she saw it gleaming in the sunlight a beautiful black opaque coloured jewel. She ran in its direction and on reaching it came to an abrupt stop. She placed both feet firmly on the stone so that the audience could be in no doubt about the stone she had selected. Then drawing a long breath- she said 'Opal-this is a black stone, if you have this stone you will be more creative, inspired even and your imagination will be limitless.' The audience clapped. They were willing Ruby to complete the test successfully and the air seemed tense.

'Sapphire' bellowed Queen Diamond in the same authoritative voice.

Ruby looked to Sapphire for reassurance. Sapphire beamed an enormous smile and winked.

Her face looked to say, 'you got this.'

Ruby scanned the floor. There it was, a striking blue stone shimmering with light. Ruby rushed at the jewel and jumped on it with both feet this time.

'Sapphire, with this jewel you will be wise, intelligent and have the power of foresight but more than this you will have an ability to judge a situation very accurately. Nothing gets past the Sapphire'

Once again, she returned her gaze to Sapphire. Sapphire nodded slowly and proudly as if to say, *that's my girl.*

'Pearl' Queen Diamond announced.

Ruby had become familiar with the floor lay out and had a better idea of the Pearls location. Her running time had reduced by half. She landed on the Pearl. Pearl herself stepped forward in her typical cool unruffled manner. She crossed her arms confidently across her chest. She knew Ruby could do this.

'Pearl, this is the truth jewel-those who hold it can bring out the truth in people. It can bring about calm just as Pearl herself shows us. The Pearl makes us both loyal and sincere'

Pearl gave one slow nod of her head and stepped back into the crowd.

The excitement was building all around as the crowd began to see how close Ruby was to completing the test with all the correct answers.

'Alexandrite' she heard next

Ruby liked this one. She remembered her time with Alexandrite on Mystic Moors and used this to help her with the answer.

'Alexandrite, this jewel makes you be all that you would like to be. If you are in a difficult situation, the Alexandrite jewel will help you come out the other side without suffering. It will make you more positive about life and always look at the bright side. It helps with any medical conditions related to blood'

Ruby breathed a sigh of relief as she knew she came closer to the finish.

'Moonstone' Queen Diamond roared. She became more enthusiastic with each exercise.

Moonstone in her own unique style clumsily fell through the crowd until she reached the front. She waved frantically at Ruby with a smile which left her mouth wide open. She gave a big two thumbs up and Ruby ran to the Moonstone.

'Moonstone-for those people who would like to start a family, this is the jewel for you. It will bring you children. With this jewel, you can read minds and sometimes the future. It cannot create the future, but can tell you what the future will bring'

The crowd now began to chatter loudly around her. They were impressed with Ruby's feat of memory and were saying as much between themselves.

'Morganite' screamed the Queen

Ruby had spent quite some time with Morganite and knew its powers well. She marched to the Morganite stone.

'Morganite-this is one of the jewels you need to help you find a soul mate, a person who will bring you unconditional love. The Morganite can be a healing stone and those in its presence can be healed from stress, anxiety and depression. If you couple this with meditation it will help with all problems in your head.

'Emerald' the Queen said. Her arms now out-stretched towards the sky.

Ruby landed on the stone without hesitation. The Emerald with its striking dark green looks was easy to find.

'Best not to be around the emerald if you have been unfaithful or you will be found out. In some cases, it will make you confess! This jewel can improve your memory and for those of you who struggle with finding the right words, it will help you speak confidently and clearly'.

'Amber' Queen Diamond laughed. She smiled at Amber as if to say *this should be easy.*

Ruby glanced at her mum and raised her arms in the air showing her crossed fingers. Amber gestured back making the sign of Okay with her hand. It was her way of saying all would be okay. She knew Ruby would be exhausted and stressed. She might have benefited from a little Pearl magic herself right now.

'Amber-this is a gemstone; it is also very calming. If you are confused in any way this will give you a clear mind. If you have a strong will to do something the Amber is your best friend. It will help you to achieve'

• • •

Ruby sat down on the floor. She felt dizzy and feint and a little nauseous. She could just see the paper record of the test in Pearls hand. Pearl had been mirroring Ruby's footsteps closely so that she could hear more clearly. *It is done*-she thought-*come what may.* The whole audience erupted in cheering, changing and clapping. They waved their cloaks in the air performing a Mexican wave which travelled the whole courtyard. The noise now resembling a football stadium crowd.

Record of Test:

| Jewel | Ruby's Answer |
|---|---|
| Opal | Makes people creative, is the stone of inspiration and imagination |
| Sapphire | Makes people wise, improves intelligence, gives you the ability to see the future, gives spiritual insight, provides good judgement. Helps to calm |
| Pearl | Makes you tell the truth, makes someone loyal, enhances sincerity, |
| Alexandrite | Empowers people to be all that they would like to be. Helps solve problems and difficult situations, improves positivity of mind, purifies the blood and circulation |
| Moonstone | Makes people fertile, helps with female reproductive system, psychic abilities |
| Morganite | Can attract soul mates and unconditional love. Has the power to heal, heals stress, anxiety, depression |
| Emerald | Ability to read minds. Can uncover unfaithfulness and bring out the truth, can improve memory. Improved communication skills |
| Amber | Calming influence. Can help manifest desires, improves clarity of thought |

Ruby managed a crooked but tired smile and raised her arm in a victory punch. She felt sure they were finished and that she had answered correctly until Queen Diamond said

'Wait, not so fast…..Ruby, tell me, what is the magic of the Ruby?' She asked.

Ruby froze on the spot. She had not thought to study the full extent of the Ruby's magic. She felt so silly and began to chastise herself. Moments earlier the whole courtyard had been cheering every answer she gave. Now she could hear a pin drop. Everyone anxiously waiting to hear what she would say. She decided she must give it her best and rely on all that she had learned about the Ruby so far.

'The Red Ruby of Braeriach is my Ruby. I am sooo blessed to have this jewel. My Ruby has the power to make friends of enemies, and make friends, better friends. If you are tired, like me right now, it will replenish your energy levels. It is a caring jewel. For those who struggle with money, it can make you wealthy. It can improve the generosity of those people surrounding you. It can protect the home and allow dream interpretation. It will banish bad dreams and create only good ones. My jewel is my precious jewel and I love it with all my heart' Then Ruby scrambled to her feet with her last ounce of energy and bowed to Queen Diamond.

The whole room broke into a cheer. They were so proud of her; she really had done well under extreme pressure. Suddenly another two bright lights appeared at the entrance to the courtyard. Queen diamond held her hand in the air to command silence.

'Morganite, how nice of you to join us and who is this? She inquired.

'My apologies Queen, I hope I have not missed too much. My guest has not travelled by the light before and was having difficulty with the meditation, but I needed to bring him here to right a wrong. This is Professor Clapton; he is the one true love of Amber. They were separated long ago because of the Black rain and'

Queen Diamond held her hand up once more.

'I know the story, why is he here?'

'To bring you the cure for the black rain my queen'

Then Amber stepped out of the shadows on the balcony.

'Charles?' She said softly using his Christian name.

Professor Clapton looked up, tears streaming down his face

'Amber, my love'

Amber alighted across and onto the balcony and into the courtyard where their lights merged together as if dancing with each other. The whole room danced and clapped with them. Queen Diamond smiled. She looked genuinely delighted that they had found each other again but she thought they may have all overlooked why they were here.

'Please, please' she said assertively.

'This is a beautiful moment and I will only interrupt it for one second. Sorry to break up the party. I would like to remind us why we came. I would like to officially pronounce Ruby, Ruby the White Witch of Braeriach. Congratulations Ruby'

The whole court began to chant

'Ruby, Ruby, Ruby'.

Queen Diamond continued.

'Just one more thing. There is something you may have missed Ruby. A minor omission about the powers of the Ruby. Those who hold the Ruby know it to be the jewel of royalty and I always remind every new White Witch that I have been searching for one hundred years for the next queen of the White Witch Coven. With the right mentor, preparation and guidance perhaps this could be you Ruby?' The whole courtyard gasped. Moonstone whispered

'You do know the White Witch queen can marry whomever she wants too. You could marry Daylin?'

Ruby had remembered and, in truth, it had been her first thought.

'Don't be silly Moonstone, honestly!' she said, diverting her gaze to the floor so that Moonstone would see how much she would like that to happen.

Amber drew closer to Charles's once again and said.

'Imagine that. Our daughter the new White Witch Queen?'

Charles's' light fell to the floor as if he had passed out. He then floated back up and recovered himself.

'You mean...... Ruby is my daughter?' He asked in an elated voice.

'Yes Charles. Ruby is OUR daughter'.

Charles started to laugh and cry all at once. His heart filled with joy and he began to shake. He was bursting with an emotional cocktail of love and pride. He could barely form a coherent sentence, and it took everything he had, to say what he needed to say.

'Amber, I know I let you down and, it might be a little too late for both of us, but, well, would you do me the honour of becoming my wife. Amber, will you marry me?'

The End

# Acknowledgements

Thank you to all children known and unknown to me who inspired the writing of this novel. I hope it gave you a place to escape to.

A sincere thank you to Kary Oberbrunner, the Author Academy Elite team and The Guild editorial team (Gailyc and Abigail) for being my guiding light during the writing of this novel.

It has been an absolute pleasure to work with Andrea Orlic on the cover design. A truly talented designer. Many thanks.

A special thank you to one of my beta readers my amazing daughter Talia McMillan.

Thank you to Muncaster Castle for hosting my book signing launch.

Thank you to my wonderful son Niall Highton who worked so hard trying to promote my book.

# Back Advertisements

If you would like to know more about the author, or more on the White Witch series, please join the authors Facebook Group S.E.Aitken

The author is available to make visits and perform motivational talks on the novel, diversity and mindfulness. If you would like S.E.Aitken to perform a talk-please make contact through the Facebook Group S.E.Aitken.

Printed in Great Britain
by Amazon

76346233R00149